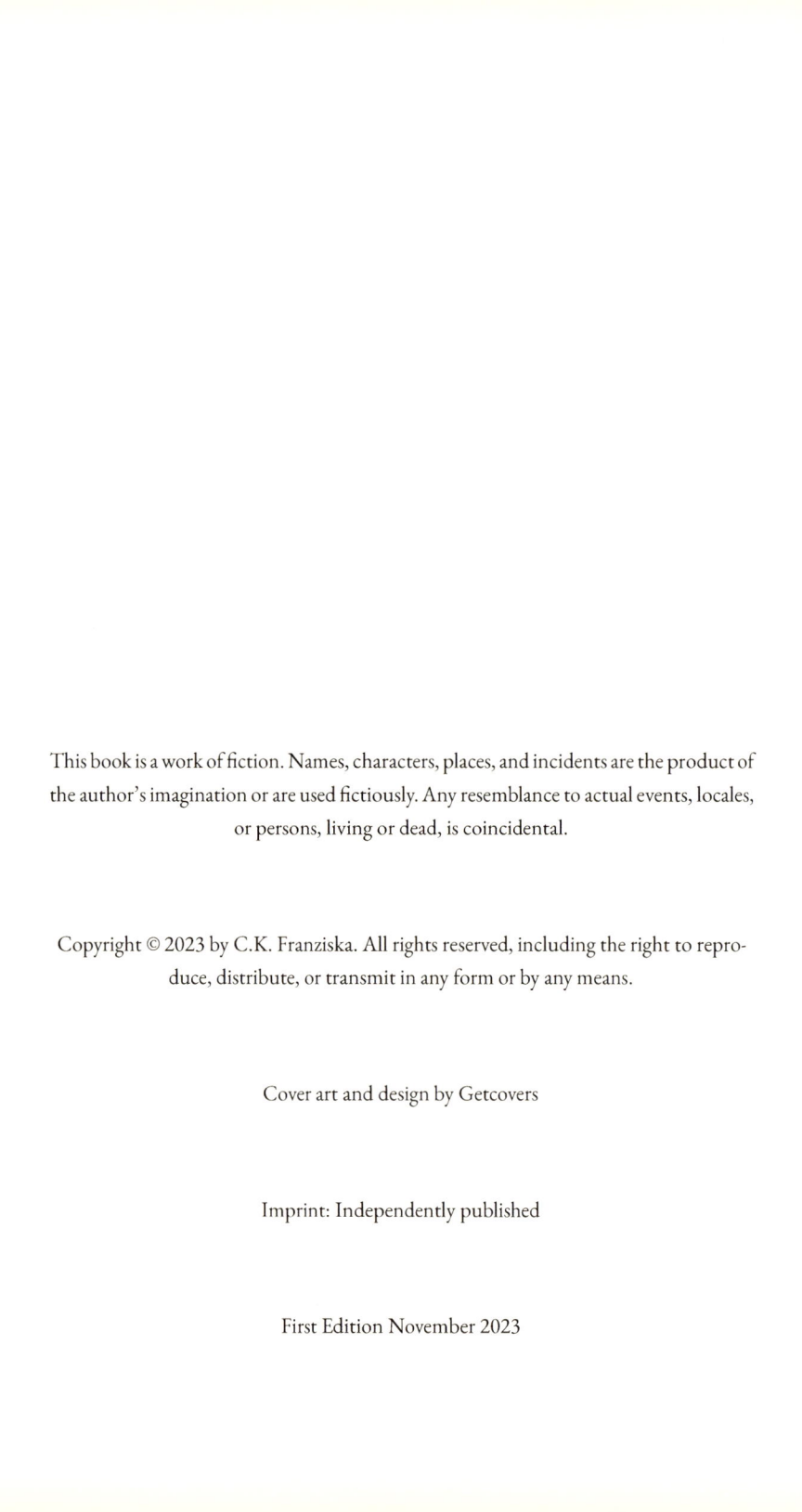

This book is a work of fiction. Names, characters, places, and incidents are the product of the author's imagination or are used fictiously. Any resemblance to actual events, locales, or persons, living or dead, is coincidental.

Copyright © 2023 by C.K. Franziska. All rights reserved, including the right to reproduce, distribute, or transmit in any form or by any means.

Cover art and design by Getcovers

Imprint: Independently published

First Edition November 2023

MORE FROM C.K. FRANZISKA

A Speck of Darkness Series:
A Speck of Darkness
A Speck of Dawn

The Crymzon Chronicles:
Monsteress
Hunteress

Be the beacon of light others are drawn to, but never mistake your kind-heartedness for weakness.

GUIDE

Places
Shadowmyre
Underworld
Darklands
Caves beneath the Underworld for souls without chance of redemption

Houses of Sins
House of Lust
Avira/Temptress
Isabella Sternling/Mother of Lust
Lysander
House of Gluttony
Oliver Voracious/Feast Beast
Olive
House of Greed
Madison Avarice/Gold Gobbler
Ruby
Gavin
House of Sloth
Ethan Lethargy/Lazybones
Desiree
Sawyer

C.K. FRANZISKA

House of Wrath
Victoria Fury/Fury
Ryder
House of Envy
Lucas Green/Green-eyes Monster
Ava
House of Pride
Sophia Hubris/Ego Titan
Leo

Other characters
Netherius
Prince of the Underworld
Mordecai
Beaked Dragon
Emberix
Fallen Dragon
Maeve
Healer
Malian
Keeper

PROLOGUE

Otyx

Have you ever wondered what happens to your soul after your body runs cold?

I bet you're imagining your afterlife in the clouds, close to the sun and far away from darkness.

That's where you are wrong.

What if I tell you that every single one of you carries darkness inside them? What if I tell you I'm called whenever a soul is ready for collection?

It's easy to figure out which sin your soul leans on. Maybe it's pride or gluttony. It could be sloth, greed, or envy. My personal favorites are wrath and lust.

You might wonder why. It's simple: those two sins seem to intertwine effortlessly.

Every time a mortal is about to expire, I'm called. It's quick and somewhat painless. At least, that's how it was until I was called for one soul in particular.

None of my virtues seemed to react to the soul I needed to collect. But it should have. Mortals love to sin. It's their nature.

Only a few mortals go to the God above—Zorus. So few that I'm surprised that this soul is trying to slip through my fingers.

After trying the sins over and over again without success, I usually would release the soul to Zorus so it can claim its place under the sun.

But greed, oh sweet greed, can be so tricky. Or maybe it was envy that overtook me.

In the end, it doesn't matter. All I know is that she's with me now, and whoever is trying to take her from me will have to go through the Underworld and me first.

ONE
Avira

"Isn't it your turn to enter Nekrojudex?" Ruby asks, inspecting my tools closely.

"I hope not. Do I look like someone who can fight her way through the trials?" I ask, attaching the last piece of the golden fabric to the dress before me. "And stop with your sticky fingers. The last time I invited you into my room, I was missing more than half of my stuff."

Ruby leans back, but her eyes are glued to the shining pair of scissors before her. "That could've been anyone," she says, licking her lips as she sits before me, her ashen skin resembling a canvas drained of color.

I let out a laugh and pull my belongings spread out over my table closer to stop her temptation.

It's difficult for Ruby. I mean, greed is the sin that brought her here.

I'm unsure how I made it here. One moment, I'm happy—I think—and in the next, I grabbed the hand of the most unusual man I've ever seen. Even though that's almost one hundred years ago, it feels like yesterday when I looked into his dark eyes for the first time.

Otyx, the God of the Underworld, has the ability to see into the depths of a soul, and he passes judgment accordingly. Judging a soul seems like a pretty big deal to me, but he made it look so easy.

I can't recall if I feared trusting the God with my soul because he's all I remember from my past. His soft, ethereal hand, the shadows and smoke enveloping him, the smile he gave me when it was my time to go.

"Did I tell you that your mother wants to see you?" Ruby asks casually, and I drop the thread and needle in my hands.

"What?" I gasp, pushing the dress back into the box to hide it under my bed.

"It slipped my mind. But yes, she wants to see you."

I've been waiting for this day. No. I've been dreading this day. With Nekrojudex around the corner, the century games to elect a new Head of Sin, I'm almost sure what she wants from me.

As her favorite daughter, she wants me to claim a place as one of the Seven. Even though I've proved over and over again that I'm not keen on joining Nekrojudex, she insists on it.

"You need to go," I tell Ruby, pushing her out of my room.

"But the scissors," she whispers, looking over her shoulder to see them one last time as her short white hair covers her big, expressive eyes.

"Are mine," I grin, pulling the door shut behind us before locking it with a key I keep around my neck. Without this safety measure, I'm sure my room would be emptied every time I left.

"So, what are you going to tell her?" Ruby asks, finally making eye contact for the first time since she burst into my room.

I watch my friend grin at me. Her skin is as gray as her clothes, her eyes big and round, and her hair short and white as paper.

"That I'm not interested in being a contestant. Honestly, they will kill me in the first round."

Yes, you can die here. I guess *banned* is a better word for it because no one wants to live an eternity on the second floor in the Darklands. I've heard it feels like a continuous circle of dying.

"I can see it. Avira the Temptress," she says, smiling as she paints my new name into the sky.

"Don't be ridiculous. If...and I mean *if* I have to join Nekrojudex, I won't go after my mother," I cut in, walking towards the center of Shadowmyre, where the palace towers above the land.

"I didn't say you should kill her. You can claim any other sin and give yourself a new name. But I thought Temptress suits you."

"I think Avira sounds just fine," I answer, ignoring the other souls walking past us.

As we stride through the nightmarish realm where the architecture defies all logic, my eyes fall on the ominous Seven-Pointed Star, a structure as ancient as sin itself. Each of its seven points, akin to a colossal spire, represents a cardinal sin, and they reach out into the abyss like accusing fingers.

The star's ghastly points loom above us, shrouded in shadows that seemed to writhe and whisper accusations. My heart pounds as we walk toward the point where the sin of lust resides. My mother, long lost to the Underworld's seductive grip, awaits me there. But why?

In Otyx's name. Stop asking stupid questions you know the answers to, Avira, I think, quickening my pace.

Our footsteps echo in the desolate silence as we approach the House of Lust's corner. The very air seems to thicken with a palpable, otherworldly desire that claws at my mind and heart. I feel the pull, the relentless temptation that this sin exerts upon me, and I cling to my determination like a lifeline.

Ruby, the first friend I found the day I got here, is no stranger to temptation herself. Her sin, as palpable as the lust surrounding us, is greed. Yet, here she is, standing by my side, her unwavering loyalty a beacon of light in the darkness.

"You don't have to come with me," I say, forcing a smile on my lips.

"Are you kidding? I want to be the first to know you've been selected. I've been dreaming of cheering you on since Otyx brought you to Shadowmyre."

As we reach the intersection of lust and my destination, I can't help but glance at the seductive sights that surround me. Sultry whispers and seductive laughter waft on the unseen winds, drawing my gaze to the undressed dancers whose forms shimmer like mirages in the dimly lit void. Their eyes, filled with an insatiable hunger, seem to beguile, and beckon.

"What would I give to have them just for a night?" Ruby whispers, coming to a halt to stare at them. "Maybe two or three nights, just to make sure."

"Stop it," I say, grabbing her hand to pull her away.

I'm here for a purpose. I tighten my grip on Ruby's hand and press forward, past the alluring distractions, until we reach the center of the House of Lust. A colossal palace looms, a fortress of shadowy grandeur pierces the heart of the star's seventh point.

As we enter the palace, we walk through a veil of an oppressive sense of power, and the walls seem to watch, adorned with twisted carvings that depict the tragic tales of souls ensnared by their vices.

I don't need long to find her—Mother of Lust—imprisoned in a gilded cage of her desires. Her once-vibrant beauty has faded into a haunting pallor, and her eyes, once filled with fire, are now vacant and empty. My heart shatters at the sight.

"Mother of Lust," I whisper, tears stinging.

She turns, her gaze meeting mine with a flicker of recognition amidst the emptiness. A faint smile tugs at her lips, a glimmer of the love that has been stolen from her.

"Avira," she says, her voice full of hope. "You're finally here."

I used to come here daily to speak to Isabella. Since I can't remember a single moment of my past, I always hoped she could guide me in the right direction to find out who I am, or rather, who I was before entering Shadowmyre.

But over the years, I had to learn that no one recalls any parts of their past. Once you take Otyx's hand, all your memories are wiped clean, and the only thing you're left with is the name he gives you and your primary sin.

I would never say out loud that he made a mistake. He's a God. But somehow, deep down, I feel like he messed up. Did lust really bring me here? For how repelling the daily orgies and naked dancers make me feel, I believe he was wrong for putting me into the House of Lust.

"Say something," Ruby whispers, bringing me back into the palace. "She's waiting for you."

"Mother," I say, swallowing down my tears. "How can I help you?"

I know how I should help her. I should take her by her hand and pull her out of the cage she built around herself. Would it be easy? No. It might take some time until lust loosens its grip around her, but I know she can do it.

But she doesn't want to leave her cage. That's the real problem. Just like everyone around me, she accepted the way Shadowmyre works.

"It's time," she says, reaching through the bars in my direction.

"For what?"

"You know what," she says, pressing her face against the golden bars to move even closer.

I shake my head but keep a slight smile on my face. "Instead of participating in Nekrojudex, I've decided to make a name for myself," I blurt out, pressing Ruby's hand. She winces under my touch until I ease the pressure. "What do you think about the name Temptress?"

My mother studies me, and I see the spark inside her eyes reignite at that exact moment.

"Temptress?" she asks as the corners of her mouth lift.

I furrow my brows and look at her. That's why she brought me here, right? To tell me I have to step in front of Otyx to fight for a seat amongst the Seven?

"That's correct," Ruby says, bowing before her. "Temptress."

What is she doing? We don't bow before the Heads of Sins. Ruby has been in Shadowmyre way longer than I have, and I've never seen her bow before Madison, the Head of Greed.

"That's the best news I've heard for a long time," Isabella says, curling her fingers around the bars, and I watch with wide eyes as she bends the metal to form an oval shape into her cage. "Temptress, huh? That's not bad."

The woman stepping out of the cage is nothing like the one I've been avoiding for weeks. Did she play with me? Was this all a big scheme I couldn't figure out?

"Oh, don't look so surprised, my child," my mother says, walking in my direction. "This took way longer than I expected for you to step up. You're meant for more than just tailoring clothes."

I shake my head. "I was worried about you. I thought you were dying."

My mother steps closer. Her black hair thickens, turning back into the wavy mane I'm used to. "Dying? I'm already dead. Yet, I don't think I could have handled another day without touching another soul," she says, brushing her hands over Ruby's arm.

With each stroke, her beauty restores as she feeds off Ruby's lust for her. Living in a cage for weeks, depriving herself of physical touch, was the method Isabella chose to get me to join her House of Sin. I should have known. After all, scheming and sins are all this place is.

"Do you want to tell me more about how you want to make that name for yourself?" she asks, letting go of Ruby.

My friend flutters her eyes at my mother as she speaks. "I thought she could coax Otyx out of his shell. I mean, why not aim for the big guy?"

I choke on my spit. "Excuse me?"

No. That won't happen. I won't march up to the God of the Underworld to persuade him, not over my corpse—jokes on me.

"I like that idea. But let's start small. Otyx is the endgame. You should start with Netherius."

Revolted, I step back. "I won't sleep with a God nor the Prince of the Underworld," I say, my voice steady.

"Then what's the point?" my mother asks, braiding her raven black hair into a butt-long braid.

"If I do this, I'm going to do it my way," I say, looking around the room. I need something, anything, to get me out of this situation.

"And if you don't do it, I will send you to the trials. Tonight is the Nekro-Ball, and if I don't see you making a move, I will ensure you're picked to represent the House of Lust."

I throw my hands in the air. "I don't even have a dress," I say, looking at my friend for support.

"The golden one would suit you just right," Ruby says, and I bite my lip.

"It's for Desiree," I answer, looking at my mother to see if she heard Ruby mentioning the dress. Of course she did.

"Just take it. She won't mind. It's technically still yours since you're the one making it," she says, strolling away from us. This is her way of telling me that our conversation is over.

"I can't," I say, stomping my foot to get her attention.

Isabella is right. The dress is still mine. Desiree doesn't know it exists because I meant to surprise her this evening when she came to get dressed for the Nekro-Ball.

But I can't take it from her. It's wrong. I put my heart and soul into the gown to make my friend look good. Primarily because she represents the House of Sloth as one of the youngest souls and because I want to light up her mood. Maybe if all eyes are on her, Ethan, the Head of House Sloth, will change his mind to select her for Nekrojudex. Even if her chances are slim, I have to try.

The wicked smile on my mother's face tells me I'm about to get the short end of the stick. "Leave it to me."

TWO

Avira

It should surprise me to find out that Desiree vanished. While everything points at my mother, I can't be sure because stuff like this happens all the time in Shadowmyre. Just because we're in the Underworld for eternity doesn't mean we're safe here.

"I've never seen you this depressed," Ruby says, helping me into the dress while I watch her pocketing one of my thimbles.

"I'm not depressed. I'm nervous. It's my first time facing Otyx since he took me."

"There's nothing to worry about. He won't even notice you're there," Ruby says, tightening the strings on my back. "Just stick to the plan. Get the Prince's attention, and before you know it, you can call yourself Temptress and get out of Nekrojudex."

That's easier said than done because I shine the brightest in the sea of souls. At least, that's what I call it. Everyone around me, Ruby and my mother included, walks around in black and white and every nuance in between. I haven't seen another colorful soul down here since I can remember.

"This color looks stunning on you," Ruby says, pulling one more time as I gasp for air.

"Desiree would have loved it," I whisper, trying to breathe.

"She would have drained the color right out of it," Ruby says, stepping away from me, and her eyes are already resting on the shiny pair of scissors again.

I need to lock them away somehow. Not because I don't want Ruby to take them, but because it's my last pair, and I don't know if I'm lucky enough to find another one on the outskirts of Shadowmyre.

"This was a mistake," I say, stepping away from the suffocating sight of the ballroom doors. "I shouldn't be here." I take one more step and then another.

"Where are you going?" Ruby asks, holding her hand in my direction.

"I can't do this," I say, shaking my head. "I'm not ready."

"No one ever is. Just take my hand, and let's get it over with," she says calmly, pushing her hair behind her ear.

When she moves in my direction, my body goes into flight mode. I turn on my heels and bolt through the souls following us, elbowing my way against the stream.

I'm not meant to be here. Otyx has to be wrong. He must. Through the crowd, I can see the palace's entrance doors. I'm so close. Then, I see my mother. Her eyes are directed to the high ceiling, threatening to land on me next. I come to an abrupt halt.

No. She will announce me as a contestant if she sees me fleeing the palace.

Frantically, I look around. I need another way out.

My gaze falls on a door to my left, far away from overdressed souls. There. I will hide in there until the entrance hall is empty. Then, once the entrance hall has cleared, I will leave.

My heart hammers in my chest when I rip the door open and slam it shut behind me. Exhaling, I press my back against the door and am about to sink to the floor when I see them. Soft rays of light filter through heavy velvet curtains, casting a gentle glow upon the carefully arranged mannequins displaying a collection of impeccably tailored suits.

As I stand there, my heart momentarily stolen by the sight before me, my gaze fixates on a particular suit that hangs upon a wooden frame with a presence that commands the room. It's a masterpiece, a symphony of fabric and design. The suit is a deep shade of midnight blue, a color that exudes confidence and mystery. Its material, a luxurious blend of wool and silk, catches the light in such a way that it shimmers like a moonlit sea. The cut is impeccable, with sharp lines and clean edges that accurately accentuate the male form. The trousers taper gracefully, and the jacket hugs the shoulders just right. It's a suit that whispers of power, of timeless elegance.

I can't stop marveling at the details—the silk-lined lapels, the carefully chosen buttons, and the expertly stitched seams. It's as if this suit has been tailored with a singular purpose in mind: to embody perfection itself.

As I approach the work of art, a soft rustle of fabric beside me catches my attention. I turn slightly, my eyes widening as I see him standing in the room's shadows. A man wearing a pitch-black suit, tall and enigmatic, has his back to me. No, it's not black. It's the same fabric I have been marbling over.

He looks to the side, and his hair cascades in a dark, silken waterfall down to his shoulders, his rugged stubble framing a strong jawline.

I watch as he slowly turns to face me. Like pools of mystery, his dark eyes lock onto mine, and for a moment, the world around us fades into insignificance. Those eyes, deep and penetrating, seem to see straight through me as if they hold the secrets of a thousand lifetimes.

The man's expression is inscrutable, his gaze unwavering. His lips part as if he's about to speak, but no words emerge. Instead, his eyes narrow slightly, a hint of curiosity mixed with something I can't quite decipher.

I feel exposed under the weight of his gaze, and yet there's an undeniable recognition. How do I know him?

As the seconds tick by, I blink, lower my gaze, and step back. "I'm so sorry. I didn't mean to interrupt whatever you were doing," I say, my voice shaking.

I hear the clicking sound as his lips part to answer, but I don't wait for it. I open the door and rush out of the room into the souls mingling before me. The funnel of excited souls drags me into the ballroom, and when I see Ruby standing in the middle of the room, searching for me, relief washes over me.

Who was he, the man in the exquisite suit? What stories hide behind those dark, searching eyes?

"Where did you go?" Ruby asks as I come to a screeching halt before her.

"I just needed a minute," I answer, breathless.

I know one thing for sure: I'm captivated, drawn to a man I've never seen before, a man who seems to...have a room in the palace?

Ruby waves her hands in front of my face. "What are you thinking of? You spaced out for a second."

Gasping for air, I grab her shoulders. "I think I just met Netherius," I mumble as my knees shake.

THREE

Avira

The ballroom is bathed in an aura of sophistication and overly crowded by souls trying to mingle with each other.

I've only been here a minute, and I watched a man walk by, his plate so full that he had food stuffed in his mouth to carry more. I saw another soul trying to steal a bunch of forks while in the corner, a herd of souls moaned into each other's ears as they rubbed their bodies against each other.

On a regular day, I would blend it out. I would walk past it, paying it no attention. But here, cramped into a ballroom, there's no escape.

"Let's grab a bite," Ruby says, pulling me on my arm to the table covered in delicacies. "I know we're supposed to dance and do all this boring stuff royals do, but I'm starving."

I don't have enough willpower to fight her, so I let her drag me toward the delicious smells that make my mouth water.

"How did you get an invitation?" I ask Ruby, who's already elbow-deep in a roasted pig.

"I still had a few favors unfulfilled," she says, biting into a serpentine sushi roll, and my face crunches, thinking about the creatures in Shadowmyre's rivers. "Plus, I couldn't let you go alone. I mean, hello? What are you going to do without me?"

Seriously. What would I do without her? It never crossed my mind. The second she saw me moving into the room beside her, she stormed my place to meet me.

"I'm glad you're here," I say with a smile as I hesitantly grab one of the forgotten fruits, a lava-grilled steak, and a glass of soul-infused nectar.

"Besides eating and dancing, what is the point of the Nekro-Ball?" I ask, walking beside Ruby to a secluded opening beside the dancefloor.

"You're still so young," Ruby laughs, and I step to the side to dodge the food flying out of her mouth. "The Heads of Sins will announce their contestants at the night's end. Each House has selected a soul for Nekrojudex. Only the best of the best get to enter the trials."

My stomach bottoms. Did my mother really think I was ready to go up against the best of the best? I'm more of an average type of soul on a good day.

"Don't worry," she says beside me, elbowing me into my ribs. "Isabella won't send you. Even though you are her favorite, you suck at fighting."

"Ouch, thank you," I say, glaring at her.

"Everyone knows that," she mumbles, stuffing another sushi piece into her mouth.

"Keep ramming that knife into my heart," I giggle before taking the first bite of forgotten fruit. It's sweet and juicy. My eyes roll back when I take another bite. How have I never tried this before? It's divine.

"Ruby?" a man asks as he passes by. "I thought you didn't want to come."

"Oh hey, Traver. I changed my mind."

I look back and forth between them. Traver? Ruby never mentioned a *Traver* before.

"Would you like to dance?" he asks as Ruby fills her mouth again.

She looks at me, at Traver, and then at me again. "You mean me?" She points at herself and swallows without chewing.

"Yes," he smiles, stretching his hand out.

"Is it okay?" Ruby asks, looking at me for approval.

"Of course. Have fun." I grab the plate out of her hand. "I won't leave."

Ruby grabs his hand, and they are on the dancefloor within a heartbeat.

Poking in my food, I watch Ruby twirl through the ballroom, clinging to Traver like a vine.

"They look like they're having a great time," someone says beside me, and when I twist my neck, my knees wobble. "Why aren't you out there?"

"I'm just waiting for my friend to return," I answer as the Prince of the Underworld stirs his glass with his finger.

"*Friend?*"

I point at Ruby as she dances and laughs with one of the most peculiar souls I've seen here. "She's right over there."

As if she senses the cue, she bends her neck in my direction and gives me the biggest smile.

"That's impressive. I didn't know souls still befriend each other."

Still? What does he mean by still?

Pressing my lips together, I find my courage. "I'm sorry about bursting into your room. I didn't mean to disturb your alone time."

"Who says I was alone?" he asks, smiling at me.

"I-I didn't see anyone else."

"You didn't notice me either," he says, and an icy shiver runs down my spine. "I'm just messing with you," he continues, fumbling with the black button on his sleeve. "Would you like to dance?" he asks, holding his other hand in my direction, and my heart almost jumps out of my chest. "It's the only way to make up for your mistake."

"I would rather—"

I see my mother's burning eyes on me. It's so uncomfortable that I grab the Prince's hand and smile at him. "I would love to."

If I don't dance with Netherius, my mother will win. Not only was Desiree's disappearance for nothing, but I will also end up in

Nekrojudex if I can't convince Isabella that I'm working on my name.

"Avira, right?" the Prince asks, pulling me onto the dance floor.

My eyebrows furrow. "How do you know?" I ask, watching the grin on his face widen.

"Let's just say that the God and I share a special connection. He might be the immortal collecting the souls, but I keep them in line."

Ruby rushes past us, and when she sees my partner's face, her mouth pops open. I can see the words *Are you kidding me?* form on her lips before her partner twirls her out of sight.

I wish I were kidding. Somehow, I ended up in the Prince's arms without even trying. Maybe he noticed me because I didn't look remotely interested in joining the fun. Or because I stormed his chambers.

"Do you know how to dance?" he asks after I step for the fourth time on his polished shoes as I try to keep up with his steps.

"I'm a natural," I grin, stepping on his toes again. "No, not really."

He laughs, and more eyes fall on us.

"You look like you were born in a palace," he muses, taking in my long blond hair and dark golden eyes.

"I wouldn't know. I remember nothing of my past."

"Is that so?" He cocks his head. "To me, you look like a princess. A golden star amid the gray night sky. An angel so bright no one else can compare to."

My stomach flutters, and I grasp for words that won't come.

He raises an eyebrow. "Too much?"

I shake my head, stepping on his toes again. "I'm just a normal soul, like everyone else. Just because my skin still glows doesn't mean I'm any different from them."

I want to run. Far, far away.

"But you are, and deep down, you know it," he says, pushing me away to pull me closer again.

I know that. I've waited for my color to drain like everyone else's, but here I am, still warm-colored and blonde.

But that's not the point. Even if I take longer to adjust to Shadowmyre, I'm still as damned as the rest.

"Why would *he* erase our memories to begin with? Wouldn't it be more wicked to let us remember how we ended up here? Or the thought of everyone we left behind? The people who mourn us?"

Netherius looks at me. "I don't think the souls mind it. Look at them. Do they look like they are missing their past?"

My eyes wander over the grayish people gawking at us. No, they seem okay to me. But I'm not. I want to know.

To change the subject, I point at the obsidian throne towering in the middle of the room. "Where is the God?"

Netherius looks over, and his eyes narrow. "Oh, so you're here because of him," he says, looking down at me. "He was here just a minute ago. I think he finally took the time to approach the soul he has been dying to meet again."

Just the thought of a God being interested in a particular soul makes me cringe. Doesn't he have more important things to do? Doesn't he have souls to collect and people to damn?

I swallow. "I didn't know—"

"That Gods have feelings, too? It's hard to wrap your head around, isn't it? I'm unsure if they can experience deep emotions, but I want to believe they can."

"Can you?" His eyes widen at my question, and I freeze when those words cross my lips. "Don't answer that. It doesn't matter."

But *can* the Prince of the Underworld feel emotions and not just the emptiness the souls around me experience?

"Never apologize," Netherius says, leaning closer so his mouth is beside my ear. "I can feel your hand in mine. I can feel your warmth seeping through my suit where you touch my shoulder. And I can feel sparks inside me every time you smile."

My heart hammers so loud in my throat that I almost choke on it.

When he swings me around, my eyes lock with Ruby's. She stands at the far end of the dance floor, waving so hard at me I can't do anything but grin at her.

"You're breathtaking," the Prince says, pulling me in again.

I feel my cheeks blush. "I think that's quite enough for a first dance," I say, straightening my shoulders to signal him I'm done.

"I'm sorry. That was insensitive of me," he whispers, leading me by my hand off the floor. "But it's hard to keep the truth to myself."

This is the moment I've been waiting for. To become Temptress, I need to make a move to keep him interested. He has given me everything I need to initiate more.

But I can't do it. It's not me. I can't play with him and use him just to my benefit.

"It's alright," I say, bowing my head. "Thank you for the dance." He lets go of my hand, and I can feel his eyes on me. When I look up, I see his almost black eyes, his hair flowing down to his shoulders with curly ends, and the stubble on his chin. He's striking, no doubt, but so is Otyx, and I know what he is capable of.

"Are you ready for the contestants to be announced?" he asks, to break the uncomfortable silence between us.

My heart hammers in my chest. Has my mother seen enough? Did this dance convince her I wouldn't be her contestant?

"Don't you think it's cruel to watch them fight to become one of the Seven?"

"Cruel?" he chuckles, brushing his curls back. "Nekrojudex gives them something to look forward to. Without it, this place would be a mess."

I never thought about Nekrojudex this way. Still, the brutal way the contestants try eliminating each other doesn't sit right with me. And even if all the contestants survive, one Head of Sins must be removed from the Seven to clear a spot.

No matter how Nekrojudex turns out, at least one soul will end up in the Darklands.

"I must go," Netherius says, gently grabbing my hand. Nervous butterflies erupt in my belly when he lifts my hand to press a gentle kiss on the backside. "We'll meet again, Avira."

I want to reply, but it gets stuck in my throat. The fine lines around his eyes cut deep when his dark eyes smile at me, and I hold on to his hand for a second to stop my knees from caving in.

Why is he doing this to me? Why now when my mother is watching me like a hawk?

Way to go, Avira. You're trying to become the Temptress just to be the one being tempted.

FOUR

Avira

"You did it! You caught the Prince's attention," Ruby screeches into my ear as I watch Netherius disappear through the door we all came through.

My heart drums against my chest as the door closes behind him. "Hm."

"That's all you have to say? How was it? Did you make a move? Are you seeing him again?"

I open my mouth to answer when the room darkens around us. The haunting strains of a ghostly orchestra cease as the souls turn their attention to something I can't see.

"He's here," Ruby whispers, clinging to my arm. She doesn't have to mention his name to give away who she's referring to.

I want to run. I need to. We can't be in the same room. I've avoided him for ninety-seven years. *Ninety-seven!*

"You look almost as gray as everyone else. What's going on?" Ruby asks, pressing herself against me.

"I need to go," I say with trembling hands.

"He won't even notice you," she whispers, looking between me and the throne.

That's the problem. He won't notice me in a sea of souls. He probably hasn't thought about me once since the day he grabbed my hand and embraced me with his wings.

But I have. I can feel his shadows curl around me whenever I open my eyes. And every night I go to bed, it's the last thing I think of. I might not be able to dream in this place, but if I could, he would haunt me in my dreams, too.

He's the key to my memories. He's the one who judged my soul and damned me to an eternity in Shadowmyre. And perhaps he's the one who can correct that mistake because I don't belong here.

"You're going to be just fine. Your mother will think you failed to draw the Prince in if you leave now. I can't let that happen."

Ruby is a lot. A thief. A liar. A hoarder. She's even greedy when it comes to sharing me with others. But she's trying. She's trying to do better, and even though her sin tells her to isolate herself and hoard everything in reach, she only wants the best for me. Somehow, against her nature, she supports me, and sometimes, less than a handful of times, she shares her belongings with me. I need to trust her because I know she's everything I got.

"In a few more minutes, all of this will be over," she reassures me, pulling me closer to the throne to hide behind a tall soul.

I don't see Otyx stepping into the room. I feel it. The ground beneath me shakes with every step, and the aura surrounding me darkens as if his presence sucks the air out of the room.

That's not how I remember him. He looked threatening, but he was gentle and quiet.

I keep my head low, waiting for the formal part of the ball to be over—*a few more minutes. I can do this.*

The only sound is my heart thundering in my chest and the sensation of my nails cutting into Ruby's skin.

What is he waiting for?

Carefully, I lift my head while the soul before me shifts his weight, revealing the man towering on the throne. Clad in robes that mirror the shifting shades of the afterlife, his eyes glint like diamonds in the dark, as if holding the secrets of a thousand eons.

The God scans the room, and my breath hitches when our eyes lock. His gaze burns on my skin as he takes me in, and one corner of his mouth lifts before he moves over the remaining crowd.

Did...did he just smirk? I must have imagined it.

I shake my head and move slightly to the side to step out of his field of vision.

His voice resonates with an otherworldly timbre that seems to emanate from the very depths of the earth. "Souls of the Underworld," he begins. "It is time for the century Nekrojudex, a tradition that has endured since the dawn of your existence. It is a tradition as ancient as the Underworld, where seven souls shall be granted the opportunity to become one of the Seven."

His words hang in the air, heavy with both promise and foreboding.

"Those chosen to fight to become a new Head of Sin shall be tasked with overseeing and maintaining the balance of their sin," the God continues. "But to earn this privilege, they must prove their worthiness through challenges as old as time itself."

I crane my neck past the man before me to catch another glimpse of Otyx. At the far end of the ballroom, atop a raised platform, stands the God of the Underworld, a figure of imposing darkness with eyes like burning coals. He's wearing nothing but a skirt. My eyes linger way too long on his abnormally muscular abdomen. Oh Gods, his abs have abs.

With a wave of his hand, seven orbs of dark energy materialize before him, each pulsating with a strange luminescence.

"These orbs represent the souls who are about to take part in the challenge that will determine their fate," Ruby whispers into my ear.

"What happens if a contestant eliminates a different sin than the House they come from?" I ask, leaning closer to her.

"Otyx will change their sin to match their new House," she answers. "Most of us reacted to more than one sin, and he let us decide which House we wanted to belong to."

Really? How am I hearing this for the first time? Did Ruby react to another sin? Did my mother? How about me?

"As the Seven, it is your solemn duty to choose and announce the contestants who will vie for one of your positions," Otyx declares. "Select your soul wisely, for their strength, cunning, and resilience will reflect upon you."

The God's gaze sweeps across the room, his eyes settling on the first of the Seven who will call out a contestant for this harrowing competition. With a beckoning gesture, he calls forth the first Head.

"Oliver Voracious, step forward," the God announces.

The first of the Seven wipes his dirty mouth with his sleeves and swallows the food he just pushed into his mouth before he moves to the God's side. I'm not shocked by his figure anymore, but surprised that the suit he wears isn't popping a seam.

"The Feast Beast at his finest. He can't even stop eating for a minute," Ruby giggles. "Let's see who represents the House of Gluttony."

I almost chuckle at the nickname Oliver made for himself. Not everyone is as lucky as Isabella. Mother of Lust is by far the best name of the Seven. Greed ended up with Gold Gobbler, Lazybones for Sloth, Fury for Wrath, Green-Eyed Monster for Envy, and Ego Titan for Pride.

"Olive will represent the House of Gluttony," Oliver says, already eyeing the food again.

I try to match the name to a soul, but when I can't recall an Olive, I look at Ruby, who's been waiting for my question.

"Olive is even more useless than you," she says, pressing her lips into a thin line. "If I remember correctly, Gluttony and Sloth have never won Nekrojudex."

"Lucas Green," Otyx barks from the throne, and I watch as the Head of Envy makes his way to the front.

"Ava will represent the House of Envy."

In this manner, the God summons the remaining Seven until they form a semi-circle beside him.

"Leo will represent the House of Pride," Sophia Hubris says.

"Sawyer will represent the House of Sloth," Ethan Lethargy announces.

"Gavin will represent the House of Greed," Madison Avarice says.

"Ryder will represent the House of Wrath," Victoria Fury answers.

"Isabella Sternling, step forward," the God says, and my knees shake.

I unhook from Ruby and step beside the man to see my mother. Her eyes find me immediately as she straightens the see-through fabric of her gown. Cold sweat forms on my skin as I hold her gaze.

She's going to sacrifice me. I can see it in her eyes. Whatever happened on the dancefloor between the Prince and I didn't convince her I could make a name for myself.

She opens her mouth, and I can barely hear her through the blood rushing in my ears. "Lysander will represent House of Lust."

My knees buckle under my weight, and the man beside me grabs my shoulder before I hit the ground.

"Thank you," I whisper, straightening myself as he stares at me. She didn't say Avira. She said Lysander. *Lysander*!

With all seven contestants announced, the God of the Underworld raises his hand once more, and the room erupts in spectral applause.

"Let's go," Ruby says calmly behind me, but I'm glued to the spot when Otyx releases the orbs to find his contestants. They stream in different directions to mark the souls for Nekrojudex.

I'm still in shock that I got out of the trials. Not only does it give me another century until the next one, but it also means that I don't have to chase the Prince anymore to keep my mother at bay. Isabella will be angry, but it will subside eventually. She can never stay angry for long—at least not with me.

"Avira?" Ruby whispers beside me, and I spin around to face her. "You ready?"

I know there must be more to his speech, but I witnessed what I needed. The confirmation that my mother chose another soul in my place. But I shouldn't feel this way—relieved. I should have accepted my mother's decision to enter Nekrojudex because now, someone else will probably be eliminated instead of me. This selfishness I just experienced, the joy of hearing another one's name in place of mine, feels wrong.

Quietly, I follow Ruby to the door, and as we steal ourselves out, my panic dwindles. It's over.

"Lysander, huh?" Ruby asks as we bolt through the entrance hall. "He's going to charm his way into the Seven."

Oh yes, he will. While his good looks and way of talking himself into everyone's pants might not affect me, I know the other contestants won't have it easy to stay on task when he's around.

FIVE

Otyx

In all the eons of being a God, I never met a soul like hers. Not only did she not react to any of the sins I offered her, but she was even too bright for Zorus.

She was a soul unlike any other, one that shined with a brilliance that defied the very essence of the Underworld.

My curiosity was piqued when I saw her, an unfamiliar sensation in a realm where apathy and solemnity are the norm. When I met her, bathed in a warm aura, her golden hair cascading in luminous waves around her, my breath stopped. She was only a young woman, her beauty untouched by the passage of time, as if she had been plucked from the prime of life and placed here by accident.

Her eyes met mine, and they sparkled with a mischievous glint, a playful spirit entirely out of place in this somber territory. She laughed, a sound like tinkling bells, and the ground beneath me seemed to shift in response.

I knew then that I had made a mistake. This soul didn't belong in this land of shadows and silence. She was a force of light and life, a presence that defied the very essence of my domain.

Yet, I couldn't undo what had been done. The laws of the Underworld are immutable, and once a soul is claimed, there is no going back.

With a heavy heart, I extended my hand, a gesture of finality, and the luminous soul took it without hesitation. She smiled, her laughter echoing in the cavernous depths as we began our journey deeper into Shadowmyre.

As we walked together, I couldn't help but feel a profound sense of sorrow and regret. I knew I had taken something precious, something that should have been allowed to flourish in the world above. I also knew that someday she would understand. Eventually, she would realize that her light was needed here, in this place of shadows and suffering, to bring solace and hope to those who had long forgotten what it meant to live.

For now, she shines as the brightest star in the darkest night, a beacon of warmth and humor in a realm that knows only cold and solemnity.

I've always kept an eye on her—always in the shadows but far out of reach.

As I look at her now, her lengthy hair bouncing in enormous waves over her golden dress, I can't help but wonder if, in the end, it's her who would save me and not the other way around.

SIX

AVIRA

I step into my room, my fingers fumbling along the wall to find the lantern and matches. I find the sandy paper, and the match strikes to life with an accelerating movement. Igniting the candle wick in the lantern, my eyes adjust to the low light, revealing a space resembling a cave of forgotten dreams. The walls, painted in a deep, velvety shade of black, absorb the light rather than reflect it. Heavy curtains, the color of the darkest forest, hang over the windows, casting the room into a perpetual twilight.

As I close the door behind me, a sense of familiarity washes over me. This room, my sanctuary, is where memories are woven into the very fabric of its existence. Not the memories I long for, but the ones I made with my friends here in Shadowmyre.

The air carries the faint scent of aged textiles, a blend of musk, and the faint fragrance of lavender sachets that line the shelves.

My eyes scan the room, pausing at the shelves filled with spools of thread, rolls of up-cycled colorful fabric, and a rainbow of buttons. Tools and trinkets sit in organized chaos, each telling a story of countless creations. I take a moment to let my gaze wander, tracing the contours of the dress forms draped in half-finished projects and the old belt-driven sewing machine, a faithful companion with years of service etched into its metal surface.

With each step, the plush carpet underfoot welcomes me, muffling my movements in its comforting embrace. It's as if the room has been waiting patiently for my return.

I kick the shoes off my feet and let my hand brush over the edge of a vintage mirror hanging on the wall, its gilded frame dulled by time. As I look at my reflection, I see not just myself but the countless hours I've poured into my craft. My fingers bear the marks of countless needle pricks, and my eyes hold the wisdom of trial and error. In this room, I tried to rediscover myself, hidden among the fabric and thread, the needle and the thimble.

I thought I could piece my memory together like I did countless times with those fabrics. Just one piece is enough to start a new idea, bringing new life to old and forgotten material.

But it turns out it's not that easy.

I move toward the center of the room, where my work table stands, a sturdy oak surface that has witnessed the transformation of many ideas into reality. A sense of purpose fills me as I pull out a worn chair and settle into it with my puffy dress.

How did I end up here? No, not in Shadowmyre, but in this dress? It wasn't supposed to snuggle me tightly. It wasn't supposed to catch the attention of the Prince. Desiree should have been the one dancing. She should have been the most beautiful soul in the ballroom, all eyes on her. Plus, if I had known that Ruby wanted to go, I would have made her a dress, too.

On the table lies a stack of old fabric, remnants of the clothes souls wore when they came to Shadowmyre. My fingers caress the worn fibers, each with its own history. As I spread it out before me, I can't help but wonder about the stories it holds and the lives it has touched before finding its way into my hands.

I wish I could remember what I wore when I grabbed Otyx's hand. Maybe it was trousers and a shirt. Perhaps I was wearing a uniform or kitchen scrubs.

What if it had already passed through my fingers?

My thoughts drift as I stare at the fabric, the memories of who I was and who I have become, blending like threads in a tapestry.

With renewed determination, I pick up the pair of scissors—luckily still in my possession, thanks to Ruby—and with precision honed by years of practice, I cut the fabric into pieces. Each snip is a declaration of my identity, a reminder of the magic that happens when my fingers dance with the material.

Someday, this will help me stitch my past back together. I know I have one. I feel it in the back of my head. But whatever I do, I can't grasp it. It's slippery and foggy.

"What are you working on?" a voice asks behind me, and I almost fall out of my chair.

"Desiree?" I whip around and trip on the dress hem as I catapult into her arms. "I thought you were in the Darklands."

"Why would I go there?"

"Because you didn't show up for your dress fitting," I say, inspecting her from head to toe.

She's still the same. Short, unbrushed dark hair and dark circles under her eyes.

"I decided I didn't want to go. It's too loud, too fast and too much work. But you look stunning. Supposedly, you danced with the Prince," she says slowly, closing the door quietly behind her.

I should have known that Desiree isn't a fan of balls. Not only does it take her an eternity to make up her mind, she also barely leaves her room. Honestly, the House of Sloth has the least amount of souls roaming Shadowmyre. Not because they are locked away, but because they choose to stay to themselves, avoiding any activities and outings at all costs.

I wave my hand. "I don't want to talk about it."

I want to, but I shouldn't. I can only think of Netherius' soul-crushing eyes and how his lips felt on my skin when he kissed my hand.

Her eyebrow curves. "So it's true?"

"I had no other chance. But did you hear the other news?" I answer to switch the subject as I return to my table. "I'm not a contestant."

"Why should you be? You're not fighting material," Desiree says, slowly making her way to my bed.

I roll my eyes. "You talked to Ruby, didn't you? Both of you could be a little more supportive."

"Supportive of something you're never going to be a part of?"

Desiree is right. This is what I wanted. So why can't I accept that I would have made a horrible contestant? Perhaps because I doomed another soul by cheating my way out of my spot.

But it's Lysander. He will be fine. I have to believe in that because otherwise, I'll go insane.

"I need to find more fabric. The least I can do is to dress him properly," I say, standing up again.

Desiree studies me wearily. "In a ball gown?"

My eyes wander over the smooth, golden fabric. *The gown*. It was meant for her, not me. "I made this for you," I answer, trying to reach the strings in the back to unfasten it.

She comes closer. "Let me help you." By the time Desiree reaches me, I could have found a way to get it off. Not only are her movements slow, but she also carefully takes in the strings before touching them.

"Just undo the knot," I say to help her speed things up, but she moves at her own pace. When the gown finally comes loose, I take a deep breath.

"I need to head back," she says, turning around to give me some privacy. "If I hadn't heard about your encounter with the Prince, I wouldn't have come."

While her sin forces her to isolate and take her time about everything she does, it doesn't affect her honesty.

"Thank you for checking on me," I say, smiling at the back of her head while holding the dress in place. Before the door even closes, I'm out of the fabric and back in my regular clothes: a shirt and pants.

If I want to create new clothes for Lysander, I must hurry. Once the contestants are announced, Nekrojudex will begin the next day. If I work through the night, I might be able to create at least one new outfit before he enters the arena. Maybe two.

Scrambling for a cloth bag, I make my way out of the door and head to the spot where every soul arrives.

The thought of receiving new clothes in the Underworld after arrival still seems bizarre. I was asked if I would like to exchange my outfit for something new, but I declined. Somehow, having just the smallest part of my past still enclosing me comforted me. Yet, I forgot what I wore the second I took it off. It's like it was the last piece of my former self that needed to disappear for my fresh start.

But most souls choose to break out of the old shell and start their afterlife anew.

"Already back?" the woman at the counter asks me when she sees me storming through the front door. "I bet that golden fabric made a beautiful outfit."

The reminder of the gown I just peeled out of throws me back into the ballroom.

No. I can't do this again. Not now.

"I can use the remaining fabric to make you something?" I offer, coming to a halt before her desk. If there's something Malian loves, it's being envious of something another person has or enjoys. That makes her the perfect keeper because nothing passes her eye.

"I won't wear leftovers," Malian says, waving her hand as she returns to her *hate list*. At least, that's what I call it. I wasn't even stunned when I discovered I made it into her top ten.

"If you change your mind, let me know," I smile, passing her to get into the room to her left.

The room is a hidden treasure trove of discarded dreams and forgotten memories. Dim light filters through dusty windows, casting a soft, mellow glow on the stacks of used clothes that line the walls and clutter the floor. It's a haven for those who see beauty in the discarded, and today, it holds particular significance for me. My mouth opens when I see all the new outfits. Otyx must have been busy collecting souls over the last few days.

I'm aware that I'm the only one digging through here, day in and day out. Somehow, I have the uncanny ability to breathe new life into old, worn fabrics. I still hope that someday I will find the clue I need to remember my past. Or perhaps I was a tailor in my past life, and that's why this place draws me in.

My eyes scan the room, my fingers itching with anticipation. Time is of the essence. I need to find the perfect fabric to upcycle into outfits for Lysander.

The room is a labyrinth of textures and colors. Stacks of discarded clothing, ranging from faded pants to vintage dresses, lay before me like silent sentinels, each holding the potential for transformation. I move through the aisles keenly, my fingers trailing over fabrics, assessing their quality and feel.

But what am I looking for? What exactly is he going to encounter in Nekrojudex? Does he need to fight his way to the top? Or is it mind games the God prefers?

My heart quickens as I unearth a pile of old tweed jackets. They are weathered and worn, but the quality of the fabric is undeniable. The tweed feels like history beneath my skin, and I know it would drape beautifully when tailored into a suit.

But is a suit too formal? Darn, I wish I would have asked Ruby for more information.

I collect several jackets, tuck them under my arm, and continue my search. That's when I spot a box of discarded silk ties, each one a vibrant burst of color and pattern. With a knowing smile, I add them to my growing collection. They will make excellent accents for the suit I envision.

What's the worst he can say? If the suit doesn't fit the occasion, I can still offer something more battle-worthy.

Time seems to blur as I gather my treasures, my mind already racing with ideas for the design.

Near the back of the room, my fingers brush against a stack of cashmere sweaters. Their softness is a confirmation of the luxury of the fabric. I imagine the comfort they will provide when crafted into a lining for the suit's interior. It will be a hidden indulgence, a secret only the wearer would know—and I.

When I pick them up, I squint my eyes to protect them from the reflection bouncing into my face. Beneath the sweaters, buried deep, I see parts of an armor. Swiftly, I grab for it, and when I try to unearth it, I'm forced to stuff my finds into the bag slung around my neck to use both arms. It's heavy. How is a person supposed to wear it without crumbling to the ground? It's a full-body armor with silver glinting metal pieces and leather.

Pushing my feet into the cloth stack, I pull on it until it wiggles free. I almost crash to the ground under the weight. But how am I supposed to carry it back to my room? I could ask Ruby for help, but that would cost me precious time.

Fastening the bag after stuffing a few more pants into it, I turn around and drag the armor behind me. That's when I see another pile reaching to the ceiling. Under closer inspection, I notice it's more black and red armor, some dented, some mangled, and just a few unscathed.

These are new. With furrowed brows, I pass the pile, remembering why I'm here.

With my arms laden, I make my way back to my room, where my sewing machine awaits. As I step over the threshold filled with discarded memories, Malian stares at me, open-mouthed. "Are you sure about that one?" she asks, pointing at the armor as I haul it past her.

"It better be worth it," I say, smiling as I lift a hand to wave at her. "I'll see you later, Malian."

She mumbles something under her breath, and I'm unsure if she's jealous about my find or if she dislikes seeing me here. But I'm her only returning customer. While the people on the surface might not be immortal like the Gods, they can live up to a thousand years. So her job is pretty easy, considering that only a soul or two need her attention daily.

As I approach my room, my steps falter. The door is ajar, a thin sliver of darkness slicing through the otherwise inviting ambiance of my home. My brows furrow with confusion. I'm certain I locked it when I left earlier.

Trying to recall my last steps before I rushed to Malian, I remember my mistake. In my haste to retrieve the fabric, I forgot to lock it.

With caution, I push the door open and step inside. My room, my sanctuary, is bathed in the same warm candlelight that filters through the lantern's glass. Everything appears undisturbed - my sewing machine sits patiently in the corner, spools of thread neatly arranged, and my tape measure hangs from its hook on the wall.

For a moment, when I entered, I feared the worst. That someone came to steal my tools, the precious fabrics, or the secrets I have meticulously stitched into my creations?

Yet, there's something amiss. A sense of unease prickles at the back of my neck. My eyes scan the room again, and then I notice what's missing - my last pair of scissors.

I approach the table, my heart pounding in my chest. They rested on my work table when I left, a striking contrast to the surrounding fabric swatches.

I take a deep breath, steadying myself.

It's just a pair of scissors.

With each passing moment, my anxiety ebbs. My fabrics are intact, my sewing machine untouched, and my designs carefully hanging on racks. Nothing has been taken or disturbed except for the scissors.

With a last glance around the room, I close the door. I've always been strict about locking it after the first break-in. After all, greed has the most amount of souls in the Underworld, and they just can't help themselves.

I drag the armor inside, drop it, and stretch my arms, taking a moment to regain my composure.

It would be easy to blame it on Ruby because I've seen her eyeballing them since the moment I showed them to her. But it could have been any soul in Shadowmyre. Getting upset over something so little doesn't feel right. Yet, I'm on a strict timeline, and if I want to finish at least one outfit, I need to get my hands on a pair of scissors.

SEVEN

Avira

Venturing to the outskirts of Shadowmyre wasn't on my agenda when I woke up this morning. But without scissors, I can't upcycle the fabric. And I can't show up to Nekrojudex without an outfit for Lysander.

Double-checking that I locked my door this time, I rush down the path that leads past a mountainous landscape to the outskirts. The longer I walk, the fewer souls I pass because no one wants to go near the entrance of the Darklands. Not even Ruby or Desiree are brave enough to accompany me when I go there.

But if I want to find scissors, I need to hurry. Walking the small trail away from the Seven-Pointed Star that makes up Shadowmyre, I vividly remember the first time I stumbled over this path, trying to find a way out. No one tried to stop me because, at that time, I didn't know that every other soul had accepted their afterlife.

But boy, did I try to find my way up to the surface. I didn't stop until I stood in front of the wall that reached so high into the clouds that it was sickening. There, I thought I found a hole that might lead me to an exit, just to halt in my tracks, when I heard the scream emerging from the darkness looming inside it.

That's where I drew the line. My curiosity challenged me to step inside, but my brain sent every warning signal flashing in red.

On my way back to the room I got assigned, I found something I didn't expect. A belt-driven sewing machine. Scattered around it, I found more sewing supplies, and without thinking, I grabbed whatever I could carry and brought it back with me. Day after day, I ventured to the same spot to find more trinkets had been added.

As I round the corner of a massive boulder to the place I know as well as my room, I discover the little treasures - a ball of vibrant yarn, a pair of dainty knitting needles, and a measuring tape.

Fueled by excitement, I pick up the yarn and needles, my fingers deftly working them into my pocket. I always wondered about the significance of these random objects in this remote location. It's as though the mountain itself has chosen me as its guardian, entrusting me with everything I need to stay sane.

Lost in my thoughts, I continue my search for the most important thing. It's then that a voice, soft as the breeze rustling through trees, breaks the silence.

"Those treasures you've found, they carry a tale, my fallen angel," the voice murmurs from the shadows.

Startled, my heart skips a beat, and I instinctively turn toward the voice. Emerging from the dimness of the boulder, a man appears, his features obscured by the play of light and shadow. He steps forward to reveal himself, his eyes locking onto mine.

"Netherius?" I ask, my voice quivering.

He offers a cryptic smile, his words dripping with enigma. "Are you surprised to find me here?"

With a deep breath, I move closer. "No, not really. This is your domain. But what are you doing here? And what tale do these treasures hold? Did you plant them here?"

But that's impossible. Until I stormed into his chambers at the palace, the Prince didn't even know I existed. There's no way he's the one sprinkling the ground with things I can use. Still, he's part of the Underworld. Even if it wasn't his doing, he has to know more about it.

His smile deepens, revealing a hint of sadness. "They're remnants of a story once woven with care and love. A story that was interrupted but not forgotten. It seems that you have been chosen to complete it."

As he speaks, the yarn, needles, and measuring tape in my pocket grow warm, as if imbued with a life of their own. Pulling them out, I throw them to the ground.

"So *you are* the one who left them here for me to find?"

His smile widens. "Oh, no. Those objects come here out of their own accord. This part of Shadowmyre is called the Dreamlands. Whatever you wish for, it will come true."

My eyes lock with a pair of scissors not too far away from us. I swear they weren't there just a minute ago.

My brain tells me to grab them and run, but I can't move. "So, why are you here? What are you wishing for?"

"That's quite personal," he says, coming even closer.

"Like as personal as the pair of scissors you're standing on?" I giggle. "You know now why I'm here." He lifts his foot, and I exhale when I notice they're still in one piece. "The floor is littered with stuff I desire, so I think it's just fair to share yours."

Netherius grabs the scissors to bring them over and stops right out of my reach. "If I tell you, you must promise to keep it a secret." The tone of his voice and the way he looks at me almost melt my knees.

I'm the worst at keeping secrets. No, that's not correct. I'm the worst at lying. But how could someone ask me about the Prince's desire? No soul is interested in that.

"Count on me," I grin, closing the space between us to snatch the tool out of his hand.

I'm so close I can smell the darkness surrounding him. It's faint and indescribable, but it's there.

"What do you know about Emberix?"

I stare at him. "Nothing. What is it?"

His curls bounce when he laughs. "I think you should see it to believe it," he says, reaching for my hand. I want to pull away, but he's faster, and before I know it, he pulls me around another colossal boulder.

"Where are we going?" I whisper, regretting my curious mind. I'm still holding the scissors. I'm not afraid to use them if he doesn't let me go soon. "My mother warned me not to follow strange souls."

He looks over his shoulder and smirks at me. "You think I'm a strange soul?"

I shrug my shoulders. "Until you prove me wrong, I won't change my mind about that," I answer.

"What could I possibly tell you for you to trust me?" he asks, walking further away from Shadowmyre. It takes me a moment to realize that he's leading me to the entrance of the Darklands. I should panic. I should pull my hand out of his and run.

Instead, I ask him all the questions that come to my mind. "Is Otyx your father? If so, who's your mother? Have you always lived here? Can you remember your past before you got here? What do you do in your free time? And where are you leading me to?"

I should have asked the last question first, but somehow, I sense he means no harm. Maybe naïveté is the reason I'm in the Underworld. Perhaps I trusted a stranger, and it ended badly.

Stop thinking about your past for one moment, Avira.

"Oh, wow. You really thought this through," he says, coming to a halt not much further. "No, Otyx isn't my father, and I don't have a mother. As long as I can remember, I've always lived in Shadowmyre. Just like you, I can't remember anything before I was created. I watch you come out here to look for your little treasures in my free time. And this is my biggest wish."

He kneels, and as he presses his hands against the iridescent surface, a hush falls over the land. Netherius closes his eyes as if his mind is reaching deep into the core of the Underworld. Responding to his command, the opal radiates with an inner light, casting a shimmering glow that spreads like ripples on a tranquil pond. The once-ordinary rock transforms into a spectacle of colors, a breathtaking display of iridescence that dances in mesmerizing patterns.

But there's more to this phenomenon than meets the eye. As Netherius continues to infuse the opal with his power, the translucent stone reveals its true nature. Within its depths, the black ground serves as a window into the very heart of Shadowmyre.

His eyes snap open, and I follow his gaze. Through the living, shifting colors, I see it—a colossal, ancient dragon, its skeletal form suspended in a state of eternal repose. The dragon's bones are as vast and intricate as the mountains, their surfaces adorned with spikes.

My breath catches in my throat as I behold it. It's a sight beyond my imagination, a creature of legend and lore. Though empty and hollow, the dragon's eyes stare back at me, and I stumble backward to escape them.

Netherius continues to channel his power with deep reverence, allowing the opal to reveal more of the dragon's form. The detailed structure of its wings, the curvature of its colossal tail, and the delicately etched patterns on its massive skull. Each bone shows strength, darkness, and a power that once ruled the Underworld.

I can almost hear the echoes of the dragon's ancient roar, a sound that reverberates through the Underworld's crust to the surface.

Netherius withdraws his hands, and the colors within it gradually subside, returning it to its ordinary, dark luster.

"Emberix is a dragon?" I whisper, taking another step back. From everything I imagined him to desire, a mythical creature wasn't one of them.

"Not any dragon. The most furious one of all," he answers, pressing himself off the ground.

My mouth goes dry. "Are you saying there are more?"

He shakes his head and stares at the ground as if he can still see her. "Not Emberix's size. She was the last one of her kind until the other Gods took it upon themselves to banish her." The hate in his voice and the darkness in his eyes are so strong that I shiver.

This isn't the same Prince I danced with tonight. He might not harm me, but Netherius is anything but harmless. I can't forget that he's still just a step below the cruelest God known to this world.

He notices the distance between us. "I'm sorry, Avira. I didn't mean to frighten you."

"But you did. Never do this again," I say, swirling my finger in front of his face.

His face softens. "I promise."

But what's a promise worth from the Prince of the Underworld? I've heard of Otyx making promises before, and every single one he broke with deadly consequences. The God might not be his father, but Netherius is like his son. They have been running the Underworld since the beginning of time.

Taking one more step back, away from the dragon and Netherius, I try to lighten up his mood. "You said your hobby is to watch me when I come out here. Is that true?"

His face whips in my direction, and the darkness masking his face immediately vaporizes when he looks at me. "Since the first day you almost wandered into the Darklands," he answers, brushing his hair back.

"Are you immortal?" I ask, searching his face.

"Aren't we all?" he counters, his eyes resting on me. "You're just as immortal down here as I am. Even though you've been down here for almost a century, you haven't aged a day."

I never thought about it that way. The eternal afterlife in Shadowmyre is the same as being immortal. My soul is trapped here and will never reach Zorus to be reborn.

Sadness washes over me, and Netherius seems to feel it. He comes closer and tilts my chin with his finger, forcing me to look up at him. "I will find a way to get you out of here."

So he knows. Netherius knows I don't belong here. But what can the Prince do? And why me? Why is he so interested in me?

Fighting every fiber in my body not to close my eyes under his touch, I take a deep breath. How did I go from never meeting Netherius before to him touching me twice in one day?

"Did you know they banned Emberix because of her wings?" he asks, releasing my chin to look back at the ground. "Every dragon with a wingspan big enough to reach the surface's crust was annihilated. The few remaining small ones live in the Darklands to stay out of the Gods' reach." He pauses for a moment to look at me. "But they didn't stop at the dragons. Every soul coming down here who possesses wings or magic is being stripped of them."

He points at the dark clouds above us, which are illuminated by the burning lights of Shadowmyre. "It's all a mirage. Above those clouds isn't a sky. It's rock. The crust to the surface where the living are."

"Why are you telling me all of this?" I ask, looking into the sky. When I look hard enough during the day, I can see the dark brown rock seeping through the clouds. I thought nothing of it because I was told where we are and why we're here. But the way he points it out, it sounds like he disapproves.

"Because I can't remember when someone spoke to me like I'm...normal. Or perhaps because after waiting for ninety-seven years, our paths finally crossed again."

My heart stumbles. "Again?"

What is he talking about? I've never met him before tonight's Nekro-Ball. At least, not that I can remember.

He's silent for a moment. "I was there when...when Otyx claimed your soul."

Something I haven't felt in years rushes through my veins. Is it fear? No, fear feels different. Hate? Too strong. Then it hits me... it's anger.

"You were there? And you just let Otyx doom me?" I can feel my cheeks heat. It can't be. I remember grabbing Otyx's hand, and no one else was there. It was just him and I. Alone.

"Why didn't you do anything?" I ask, my voice harsher than I intended.

"Because sometimes even Gods can't control their feelings."

"Feelings? Are you kidding me? Are you saying the God of the Underworld dragged me down here because he couldn't control his feelings?"

This is getting more ridiculous by the second.

"Of course not. What I'm saying is that his judgment was clouded that day."

I huff. "So I'm down here because he had a bad day? Because his mind was somewhere else when he had to do the only job he was created to do? Do you even hear yourself?"

My body is so warm it feels like years of emotions are trying to claw their way out of me. I knew it. All this time, I thought he made a mistake. And now I have proof.

Netherius presses his hands together, and I can see the muscles in his jaws tick. "Believe me, if he could correct his wrongs, he would do it."

"Oh. Is that what he told you? Guess what, I'm still down here."

I look back at Shadowmyre and the palace. Nothing stands in my way to walk right up to the God and tell him what I think about my wrongful imprisonment. Because that's what this is. He's holding me—my soul—hostage because he made a horrendous mistake.

The palace reaches into the sky like a beacon, and when I notice the sky turning colors behind it, my throat closes.

Lysander. It's almost morning.

"I need to go," I say, spinning on my heels and pressing the scissors against my chest.

"Where are you going?" Netherius yells after me, but I save my strength for running. I bolt over the opalescent ground, my steps echoing off the mountains close to me.

There's not enough time to create a suit and a battle outfit. I need to settle for one. As I reach the boulder leading to the narrow path, I look over my shoulder and my heart pains when I see Netherius glued to the spot where I left him.

He didn't deserve to be yelled at. Even if he had the guts to stand up against a God, would Otyx have listened to him?

Forcefully, I rip my gaze off him and keep running. After I hand over Lysander's outfit, I will march into the palace and request an audience with Otyx. It's something I should have done long ago, and now, with the new knowledge, it's overdue.

EIGHT

Avira

I worked endlessly through the night against the clock to finish something for Lysander. It might not be my most remarkable work, but it will do.

The cashmere sweaters now form a tailored jacket, the pants have become perfectly fitted trousers, and the leather armor serves as a concealed armor of my creation while I lined the chest with metal pieces. The blend of opulent cashmere and the armor's hidden strength reflect my inner qualities - a soft heart encased in unyielding determination.

After neatly folding the new suit and stuffing it under my arm, I rush out the door and follow the on-stream of souls leading to the center of Shadowmyre.

I made it. Now I just have to find Lysander before he enters the arena.

Brushing through the crowd, I fasten my pace. How hard can it be to find the contestants?

Moving with determined haste through a crowd of people, my eyes are fixed on the towering walls of the palace that looms ahead, and my heart races. I've heard whispers and rumors of an arena unlike any other, a spectacle that draws crowds from all corners of the Underworld. Today, I will see it for myself right before I step before Otyx to plead my case and hopefully make it out of here.

But my attention soon diverts to the center of the courtyard, where a colossal, circular hole has been excavated from the ground. I approach the precipice, my eyes widening as I peer down. The depth is dizzying; at first, all I see is darkness. But as my vision adjusts, I realize there's more to this chasm. A circular wall, covered with seats, descends from above, suspended by intricate mechanisms that defy my imagination. I watch in horror as the wall drops further, revealing a hidden world below.

Rows upon rows of spectators occupy the seats, their faces a mixture of excitement and wonder. The circular wall acts as a barrier, separating them from the arena floor below, which stretches into the abyss. It's a colossal amphitheater that vanishes into nothingness.

I can't take my eyes off the scene unfolding before me. The anticipation in the air is palpable as the spectators lean forward in their seats. They know what's coming next.

With a thunderous roar, the circular wall continues its descent, revealing the arena floor in all its glory. It's a sprawling expanse of sand and rock, marked with ancient patterns and symbols. And in the center of this arena stand two warriors, their armored forms glistening in the dim light. The crowd erupts in cheers, their voices echoing off the walls.

It's impossible. I'm too late!

As the battle between the warriors continues below, my chest tightens. This isn't just a fighting arena; it's a massacre ground.

But of course. What was I thinking? That the trials are hugging and hitting each other with wooden swords?

This is where legends are born, and destinies are tested in the most extraordinary of arenas. This is where Isabella eliminated all the other contestants and requested a battle with the former Head of Lust for the title.

Frantically, I try to decipher if Lysander is a warrior in the arena. To my luck, he's not.

Once I find my composure again, I look over to the throne standing above the wall and exhale when I find it empty. This isn't the main event. Whoever is battling down there right now is a space filler, which makes me even more nauseous.

"What do you have there?" Ruby asks, picking on the suit under my arm.

"Good Gods. I thought you would come to pick me up," I say, strengthening my grip around my creation to stop her from pulling on it. "Anyway, I need to get to Lysander to give him something."

"When I checked your room, it was locked," she says, eyeing me wearily. "You look worse than the souls in the Darklands. What happened?"

I press my lips into a thin smile. "I just really need to get this to him," I answer, ignoring her insult.

Ruby shakes her head. "The only person who can reach him now is your mother. They don't allow anyone else below the arena."

My mother. Where is she? Maybe she can help me out.

I scan the onlookers for her familiar black hair. I know she wouldn't miss this spectacle. She has been looking forward to this day since she found me stranded before the House of Lust.

But before I can move, a scream irrupts from the depths of the abyss, and when I look down, I see the head of a warrior rolling over the sand. My stomach turns so fast I have to press the suit against my face to stop me from staring at it for another second.

The crowd breaks out in cheers and screams.

Why? Why does someone think this is entertaining? And just as the tumult around me peaks, the entire arena quiets.

I hear him before I see him. With a powerful stroke of his shadowy wings, Otyx descends from the inky sky above the arena. The stone seems to absorb his essence as he touches the colossal throne, an imposing obsidian monolith adorned with ruins. They glow like the light Netherius used to show me Emberix.

From there, the God surveys the arena with eyes like burning coals. His gaze fixates on the abyssal depths below.

With a commanding gesture, he claps his hands together, a sound like thunder reverberating through the cavernous expanse. At his command, the arena clears. The decapitated soul dissipates like smoke, leaving the circular pit below empty and awaiting its contestants.

His voice, a deep rumble that resonates from the depths of the Underworld, echoes through the realm as he addresses us.

"Specters of Shadowmyre," he intones, his words sharp as the opal his domain is made of. "Today marks the commencement of Nekrojudex. A tradition that tests the mettle of souls and offers the chance to ascend to become one of the Seven."

He pauses, his dark eyes scanning the arena's depths, his shadowy wings casting a long, foreboding silhouette. "The moment has come to present the chosen contestants. And from this moment forward, be aware that if a contestant eliminates a Head, they will take their rightful place among the Seven."

My mind wanders to poor Lysander, who's about to enter the arena. If it weren't for Netherius, I would have made it in time. I could have handed Lysander the suit, knowing I did my best to protect him.

The Seven step forward one by one, their regal forms draped in a breathtaking garb that shimmers like starlight. They announce their chosen champions with solemnity and grace, each name burning into my soul.

Olive. A once blonde woman with an unathletic build, dressed in a tailored pantsuit, steps forward. Food crumbs stick to the corners of her mouth, and her fingers drive nervously over her thighs as Oliver Voracious announces her to represent the House of Gluttony.

Gavin. A soul of mature years enters next to Madison Avarice for House of Greed. He parades in a tweed suit and a neatly trimmed white beard. His spectacles perch on the bridge of his nose, and his warm, welcoming smile flashes unnatural white teeth.

Sawyer. A man sporting a faded denim jacket, tousled hair, and a carefully cultivated five o'clock shadow comes next. His gaze is fixed on the ground, avoiding eye contact at all costs as Ethan Lethargy pushes him into the arena to represent the House of Sloth.

Ryder. A young soul, hardly out of his teens, strolls in, leaving Victory Fury behind. His messy, jet-black hair and tattered leather jacket scream rebelliousness, which suits House of Wrath just fine.

Ava. A woman with wavy hair cascading down her back presses herself past Lucas Green. She wears a form-fitting dress that accentuates her hourglass figure, and her piercing eyes sparkle with mischief as she scans the onlookers with envy.

Leo. A tall man in a tailored charcoal suit steps in with Sophia Hubris. His sharp jawline and perfectly coiffed salt-and-pepper hair hint at his age. He adjusts his silver cufflinks with a subtle, confident gesture only a soul from the House of Pride can do.

But as Mother of Lust steps forward to make her announcement, a murmur of uncertainty ripples through the assembly. Her voice, soft as a whispering breeze, forces a shiver down my spine. She's never quiet and reserved.

"Isabella Sternling, Mother of Lust," she announces herself. "I've chosen Lysander, the nightshade spinner, to partake in Nekrojudex."

OTYX

Otyx observes the arena below, his gaze fixed on the seven contestants, or rather, the six who stepped forward to accept their roles. A palpable tension hangs in the air, for one of the chosen is conspicuously absent.

No. *Please, no.*

As the God of the Underworld waits for the missing contestant, a sense of intrigue and uncertainty descends upon me.

"And where might he be?" Otyx's voice bellows through the arena.

Isabella's eyes widen. "I'm...unsure."

Otyx rises off his throne, and I see my mother crumble under his presence. "Where is he?"

Isabella searches the crowd for any sign of her contestant, and when she locks eyes with me, they narrow for a split second until she turns to the God again. "I, Isabella Sternling, have chosen Avira, the Temptress, to partake in Nekrojudex."

The ground beneath me vanishes when her words carry to me.

No. She can't just change her mind. I saw the orb searching for Lysander in the ballroom. He's bound to Nekrojudex and not I. He has to be here. He has to!

Tears prickle in my eyes as the solid ground turns into quicksand, pulling me by the ankles into the Underworld's depths.

I didn't have time to prepare myself. There's no way I'm going to pass the first trial. I'm not even worth the name Temptress. So why did she use it? And where is Lysander?

The last thing I see is Otyx's eyes as his gaze meets mine, and in the millisecond, I drift between consciousness and darkness, I see a flicker of crimson in them.

NINE

Otyx

When I see the fear on her face, I want to scream. I want to use my power to stop Nekrojudex from pulling her into the first trial.

But my hands are tied.

There aren't many things that are out of my control. The return policy after claiming a soul, and the choice one of the Seven makes when choosing a contestant, are the only ones.

Until now, I never cared who entered Nekrojudex. I just sat on my throne, trying to look interested as they fought their way through the trials until one of the Seven was cut down.

But when Isabella calls Avira, I want to jump off my ass, cross the arena and make Mother of Lust pay for selecting her. She knows, as well as everyone else who ever met Avira, that she's too good to be down there fighting for something she doesn't believe in.

Hell, I don't even believe in it, but I had to do something to keep my souls entertained. If I had known that Nekrojudex could someday affect me personally, I would have never started it.

But here I am, watching as the rules I set to keep Nekrojudex run flawlessly suck Avira into the arena.

The problem isn't that I think she can't win. I fear what the trials will do to her. What if they change her? What if she becomes someone she's not? She's the only good one among the millions of souls staring at me. So good that I can't keep my eyes off her.

But I can't stop it now. She's a contestant. The only thing I can control is her chance of winning. Even better: if another contestant eliminates one of the Seven before the second round, all of this will be over.

Yet, that means that Avira has to pass the first trial.

The arena is so quiet I could hear a dropping pin. All eyes are directed at me as I scramble through all the trials I set up ahead of time.

Fuck. All of them are too much. When I created the plan, Avira wasn't a part of it. And now, it's not my choice to control the trials. Nekrojudex has a mind of its own and randomly picks from the trials I presented thousands of years ago.

Shifting on my throne, I speak to my souls as the vision of the first trial appears before my eyes. "The first trial will be *the Trial of Shadows*. The contestants must navigate through a pitch-black chamber to face a test of courage and perception. They must find their way through a maze, using only a flickering candle for illumination. Each wrong turn may lead to unsettling encounters with shadowy apparitions."

Clapping erupts around me as the arena fills with dark smoke. I might be unable to save Avira from it, but no one says I can't interfere.

"Let Nekrojudex begin."

TEN

AVIRA

Chaos breaks out above me.

Where am I?

As I look up, my gaze meets an audience of shadowy figures, their presence like whispers in the wind. They watch me with curiosity and anticipation, their faces hidden in obscurity. I feel their collective gaze weighing upon me and uneasy claws at the edges of my consciousness.

Isabella selected me. *Me!*

At first, I want to yell that this is all a horrible mistake. That we should search for Lysander and let him join the trial. But this is my chance. All night, I tried to find a way to make up for sending him in place for my soul.

The suit.

Even though I didn't have his measurements when I created it, I got pretty good at guessing. The jacket might be too big for me, but it's better than what I have on. Throwing it over my shoulder to cover the loose shirt, I feel an unnatural chill carrying through the air as tendrils of smoke swirl in my direction. I watch as my surroundings veil in impenetrable darkness until I can't see the crowd above me anymore. Actually, I can't even see my hand before my eyes. It feels surreal, as if I'm walking at the edge of a dream.

What is happening? What do I have to do?

Panic seizes my heart, and I reach out, grasping for something, anything, to anchor me in this perplexing darkness.

My fingers brush against the cool, waxy surface. Without hesitation, I grasp the candle's slender stem, and a flame ignites when my hands curl around it. My surroundings reveal a sinister chiaroscuro.

In the distance, a reddish light shimmers, its allure beckoning me. But instinct, that primal whisper in the depths of my soul, urges me to move away from it. There's a foreboding in the crimson glow, a promise of danger I dare not approach.

Slowly, I venture through the darkness in the opposite direction, my steps echoing softly in the silence. My heart hammers in my chest as I feel an unsettling sensation. Straightening my shoulders, I brush it off.

It's nothing, Avira. Remember? Whatever happens to you down here doesn't matter. You're already dead.

Then, as I walk deeper into the darkness, a haunting sound fills the air. It's the unmistakable sound of nails scraping against stone, a sinister cacophony that sets my nerves on edge. My gaze darts to the source of the sound ahead of me, and my breath catches in my throat.

I lift the candle higher, illuminating the darkness, and that's when I see it—a pair of piercing, predatory eyes gleaming in the dim light—my throat closes. Before me, a massive form emerges from the shadows. And the eyes, red and unblinking, belong to a creature of nightmares—a dragon.

ELEVEN

Otyx

What the fuck is she doing? Why is she ignoring my help? All she needed to do was to follow my light. I would have brought her to the center of the arena safely.

Instead, she walked in the opposite direction, right into the territory of the Darklands' dragons.

I need to get to her. I need to warn her and portal her out of the arena. But if I do that, I will mark her for everyone. Every soul will know that I favor her.

I'm a God. *A fucking God.* I shouldn't be doomed to listen to any rules. Rules I set up thousands of years ago. Yet, they are as binding as death.

If I do something now, my souls will think I'm weak. But Avira might be the first to be eliminated from Nekrojudex if I don't do something.

Is that really a bad thing? Wouldn't it stop her suffering before it even begins?

I can reach her in the Darklands. I can continue to monitor her, even if she isn't in Shadowmyre.

No. I need her close to me. After this trial, I will change the rules and bring all the contestants into my palace. I will put her right beside my chamber where she belongs.

My muscles twitch as I watch her.

How could I let this happen? I should have taken her to my palace the moment I claimed her.

All my muscles tense as I watch her march through the darkness. For her, it might seem like there is no light save for the candle. But from above, I can see everything clearly.

What is she doing now? Is she reaching for the dragon?

TWELVE

Avira

I hold the candle higher, my fingers trembling, revealing more of the creature's imposing form. Its scales, the color of obsidian, glisten with an unsettling radiance, and its snout—no, it's a beak—extends toward me, sharp and pointy.

The dragon's eyes bore into mine, and at that moment, all I can do is close my eyes and let the creature take me. I'm no match for a beast. I know it. The animal knows it. And everyone above us is watching this trial does, too. Even if I back away, it's hopeless. It saw me.

As the candle's flame dances and flickers in the unsettling stillness, I make a choice. I can't outrun it. Instead, I embrace it.

With measured steps, I approach the dragon, my heart pounding in my ears. Carefully, I lift my arm even when I see the sparks of fire sizzling in its throat as it opens its beak.

I can't succumb to my fear.

With a voice that almost shatters my eardrums, the dragon speaks, its words reverberating through the coldness. "Who dares to tread upon this sacred ground?" it intones, its eyes never leaving mine.

Sacred? The Underworld is anything but that.

Summoning my courage, I reply, "I'm Avira, a wandering soul. I mean no harm and seek only to find my way out of here."

The dragon regards me with curiosity, its ancient eyes piercing the depths of my soul. After a contemplative pause, it speaks again, its voice carrying an air of mystery.

"You don't belong here," the dragon rumbles, extinguishing its flame that was ready to roast me alive.

Why isn't it eating me?

My hand still outstretched, my chest constricted, I watch as it leans closer to me. The undeniable pull to touch its scales sends a shiver down my spine.

I know I don't belong. Otyx knows it, too. But I'm in Shadowmyre. Or am I currently in the Darklands? It doesn't matter. There's a reason I'm here. I might not understand it now, but it must mean something. It always does.

"You're right. I don't belong here," I say, holding my hand as steady as possible. "I have to face this trial to talk to the God."

The dragon's eyes gleam. "Talk to the God? What gives you the power to address him?"

"I'm unsure yet. But he made a mistake," I answer truthfully. "I just need to figure out how to pass this trial."

A slight rumble reverberates through the dragon's chest. I think it's laughing. "How did a mortal make it into the Underworld? And even better, how did you make it into Nekrojudex without knowing what to do?"

I shake my head. "You don't understand. I—"

Just as my fingers are about to make contact, a scream pierces the moment's tranquility. I whip my head around, my heart leaping in my chest. A man hurtles through the air toward me, his body a mere speck against the vast expanse of darkness.

In that breathless moment, my mind races, my instincts taking over. I know I must move to protect myself and the dragon, but the man plummets at terrifying speed.

"Stay behind me," I yell at the dragon, raising my arms to cover as much of it as possible.

And then, another dragon emerges from the depths of a cave. It bursts forth from the shadows like a guardian angel, its scales as dark as the abyss, and its wings unfurl with a resounding roar. With precision and grace, it intercepts the falling man.

Is that…Gavin?

I watch in shock and horror as the second dragon snaps him out of the air, its mighty wings arresting their fall. In a breathtaking display of power, the second dragon clamps its jaws around Gavin's midsection, its teeth like gleaming blades. Blood sprays across the ground, a grim reminder of the swift and brutal reality of the Underworld. It happens so fast. His scream silences abruptly, replaced by teeth meeting flesh with a bone-chilling crunch.

The air is being pressed out of my lungs as the dragon behind me steps forward, shielding me from the spectacle with its enormous leg.

When the dragon that initially held my attention moves away, its eyes reveal a depth of emotion that transcends words. Tears well in my eyes as I realize the gravity of the situation. The dragons that inhabit the Darklands are not mere beasts; they are sentient beings with their own sense of justice and order.

"He tried to eliminate me," I whisper, reaching for the dragon again. "And one of your kind saved me."

As my fingertips brush against the dragon's scaly forehead, I feel the earth's heartbeat for a fleeting moment. The dragon regards me with an inscrutable gaze, its eyes filled with fire as we connect.

"Let's get you out of here before another contestant tries to cut you down," the dragon says, scanning the darkness behind me. "This isn't a game for a mortal."

With a solemn nod, I agree. I'm in the Underworld, where the extraordinary is commonplace, where the line between wonder and peril is razor-thin.

"Mortal," it rumbles, "I'm bound to this place, as are you. But I could take you to the surface, back to the world of the living, where sunlight bathes the land."

My heart, heavy with the desire for freedom, pounds erratically. "That's impossible. Only Emberix was big enough to reach that height," I say, unable to look away.

The dragon's eyes gleam with a rare glint of emotion, a semblance of longing. "How do you know about her?"

About *her*? Emberix? The giant skeleton hidden beneath the opal on the outskirts of Shadowmyre wasn't male as I expected.

"The Prince of the Underworld showed me," I answer, reeling my thoughts back in.

The dragon tilts his head. "Only Emberix could touch the surface because we never tried it after what happened to her. For you, I'll try to reach it. But you must promise to free my family from the chains that bind us to this abyss," it declares, pulling on its legs like an invisible leash holding it in place. "Swear upon your heart and soul that you will release all of us, and I shall carry you to the surface."

I hesitate for only a moment before making my decision. The path to the surface is uncertain, but the allure of sunlight and the world above calls to me with an irresistible pull. "I swear," I answer, my voice unwavering, "I shall free you and your family from your bonds."

There's nothing left here for me. Lysander is safe from Nekrojudex, and Otyx might not have the power to help me. This is my only chance.

With a graceful movement, the dragon lowers its massive, obsidian-scaled body to the rocky ground. I should be fearful. Riding a dragon is unheard of, and the longer I think about it, the more ridiculous it feels. Yet, there isn't another way out of this arena.

I climb onto its back, my fingers gripping the ridges of its scales. They are cool and smooth beneath my touch, not as sharp as I imagined.

With the promise made, the dragon shifts, and I hold on tightly as it unfurls its immense wings, each shadowy membrane stretching toward the freedom we long for. With a powerful thrust, the dragon launches into the air, its wings beating like thunder. It rises through the darkness of the abyss, carrying me with it. The smoke gives way to a winding tunnel that leads upward.

As we ascend, the tunnel widens, and a faint glimmer of light seeps in from above. My heart quickens. I can sense the onlookers' nearness as their voices' vibration reaches me.

Finally, we breach the tunnel's exit, and I'm bathed in sunlight again. It's not the surface, not yet, but after the darkness in the Darklands, this feels like the mortal world. Blinking against the radiance, I feel the dragon's powerful form beneath me, still bearing us skyward.

But as I look around, my eyes locking onto the boundless horizon above us, I realize that my freedom comes at a cost. Sitting before me is the God of the Underworld himself, his dark eyes fixed upon me with an intensity that sends shivers down my spine.

Our journey has only just begun, and the God's presence serves as a reminder that my promise to the dragon is mere words. Why did I think this could work? Even if the dragon can reach the crust that separates us from the surface, I forgot about the Underworld's ruler.

And what will my escape do to the souls staring at me with open mouths and widened eyes? If they watch me escape Shadowmyre, what will stop them from trying to do the same?

Heat rushes through my body as I watch the God grab the armrests. Before I can blink, he launches into the air, and within the next heartbeat, he's right in front of us.

"I won't let you leave," he growls, and something invisible pulls me down as if his words drag me back to the ground.

Frantically, I scratch my nails over the dragon's scales, trying to find a grip to keep me on its back. But it's useless. The weight tenfolds and all I can do is embrace it.

Letting go of the dragon, I feel the cold air rushing past me as I fall backward into the arena. Any second, I will hit the ground and be eliminated from Nekrojudex. I will be eliminated from ever setting foot on Shadowmyre again.

My arms reach out to the dragon racing after me. I can see in its eyes that it's trying to catch me before I make contact.

It's so close...

And then, it crashes into the wall, taking a boulder out with it, as Otyx pushes it out of his way, fury blazing in his eyes.

When I close mine to accept my fate, my heart breaks for the dragon. It offered its help. And what did it get in return?

Then, the air presses out of my lungs as I hit the ground, and the same darkness I had just escaped swallows me.

THIRTEEN

Avira

"What were you thinking?" a voice barks in my head, and I jolt straight into the air.

When my eyes open, I find myself in a room carved entirely from glistening black opal. My vision swims and the echo of a haunting dream still clings to my senses. Isabella chose me to enter Nekrojudex for the House of Lust. I was sucked into the abyss before ending up in total darkness. And then there was a dragon. It offered—

Before I can fully regain my bearings, the thunderous voice shatters the silence again.

"Why?" the voice, like the rumble of an earthquake, seems to emanate from all directions, filling the opal chamber with its spite. My heart pounds as I scramble to sit up on the opal bed.

As my bleary eyes adjust to the dim light of the chamber, I see him—Otyx. He moves with a relentless, disapproving pace, his shadowy form almost blending with the inky walls. His eyes, dark as the abyss itself, are fixed on me with a withering intensity.

I try to speak, to explain myself, but my words catch in my throat. I know the gravity of my mistake. I should have never tried to escape. And for that, I'll have to face the wrath of the God.

"You thought you could simply waltz out of my domain and disrupt the order of the Underworld?" Otyx's voice drips with disdain. "You thought you could tamper with the fate of souls and evade the consequences?"

With a trembling voice, I stammer. "I... I didn't mean to... Believe me, I only sought a way back to where I belong."

His eyes bore into me with a chilling intensity. "Back?" he hisses. "And now I must clean up the mess you've made. You, a mere mortal, meddled in the affairs of the divine."

There it is again: *mortal*. The dragon used this word to describe me. Both should know that I'm just as immortal in the Underworld as everyone else. I haven't been mortal for almost a century.

He paces back and forth, his dark presence almost suffocating me. Otyx turns to face me, his eyes narrowing. "You will stay here, in this chamber, until the trials are over," he declares with a finality that brooks no argument. "And if you try to escape again, I will know."

I feel a sinking feeling in my chest. I'm trapped in the Underworld's heart, at the mercy of its God. There's no escape, no way to undo what I've done.

"How is the dragon? Is it dead?"

I should've kept my mouth shut. But it's too late.

"The dragon? Are you kidding? Why do you care about that dragon?"

"Because, unlike you, it didn't harm me."

His eyes radiate heat as they meet mine. "I've never harmed you," he growls, clenching his teeth. "And that dragon," he points out the door. "He used you as a ticket to get out of here. What was in it for you?"

"You trapped me here," I say as calmly as I can. "We both know that."

The room falls silent. I can see different emotions cross his face before he goes back to his usual coldness. "I had no other choice."

My heart skips. He admitted it. "Why? Why did you bring me here? You know I don't belong."

I cringe as Otyx picks up a vase filled with shriveled flowers and throws it against the wall. "That's what every soul thinks. No one wants to admit their true colors until death comes knocking unexpectedly."

I open my mouth and close it again.

There's so much I want to say to the God, but when he threw that vase, I realized he didn't do it because I angered him. His reaction was too severe, yet he didn't punish me for my attempt to flee. But what is causing his anger?

I'm overthinking this while already walking on thin ice.

"I didn't think it through," I say calmly, recalling the moment I got sucked into the abyss. "Everything happened so fast. And even though I knew we'd never reach the surface, I had to try. If not for me, then for the dragon."

My words bounce off him like rain on polished rock. "You will find everything you need in this chamber," he says, storming to the door. "Be ready in the morning for the next trial. And remember, if you try to escape, I will hunt you down."

The door slams shut, leaving me alone with my thoughts.

I at least expected him to exclude me from Nekrojudex. He has every right to punish me. So why isn't he? And what happened after I hit the ground? I knew I couldn't die. Still, colliding with a rigid barrier doesn't feel pleasant—*mortal* my butt. I'm just as immortally doomed as everyone else in Shadowmyre.

FOURTEEN

Otyx

I couldn't let her body shatter on the ground. As much as rage fueled me when I used my powers to chain the dragon back to the ground, I never meant for it to touch her. But my emotions got the best of me for everyone to watch.

It took little to erase those few seconds from every souls' mind. The moment I dove after Avira and wrapped my arms around her to catch her is now a blank moment for everyone involved.

Is she aware of what I've done? Certainly not; otherwise, she would have brought it up. She wears her heart on her sleeve, and even though I'm a God, she addresses me like I'm one of her friends.

The word makes me gag. *Friends.* There's no such thing. It's just people pretending to like each other just to use them for their own benefit until they either sucked them dry or they're of no use anymore.

I bite my lip. She knows too much. I need to be more careful. Apparently, erasing her memory made room for an even bigger issue: the longing for freedom. But who's really free? I know I'm fucking not.

My nostrils fill with the scent of sweaty souls, and I let out a gagging noise. After bringing Avira safely to my palace, I had to go back and clean up the mess she made. Erasing their memories was the simple part. Coming up with a lie where the seventh contestant went was a whole other.

As four out of seven souls stepped into the middle of the arena after the trial was over, I announced Avira was the first to reach the end, and as a reward, she was already on her way to claim a room in the palace.

Announcing that all the other contestants would be housed in the palace was against all my beliefs, but I had to because I'd been slacking. I was so occupied by Avira that I forgot to pay attention to the other souls. And if my judgment wasn't clouded every time she was close to me, I might have noticed Lysander's disappearance.

There are only two places a soul can go: Shadowmyre or the Darklands. And when I checked, Lysander was in neither. So where did he go? He can't just vanish. Not in the Underworld. So where is he? Someone knows something about him, and I need to find out who.

My mind wanders back to Avira. All she cares about is the dragon.

"Mordecai?" I bark as I enter the room I used for the ball. The dragon diverts his eyes to the ground, cowering before me. "You think you're so clever," I growl, scanning the corridor behind me for any nosy soul. "Look who's laughing now."

As I step inside, the door shutting magically behind me, I stride close to him. With a single, deliberate step, I extend my shadowy form until I loom over him. Like the rumble of thunder in the distance, my voice fills the ballroom as I speak, my words laced with fury.

"You sought to escape, to defy my dominion. Such arrogance will not go unpunished," I thunder, my eyes burning with an unearthly light.

With a deliberate motion, I bring my foot down on one of the dragon's colossal claws. There's a sickening crunch as the claw snaps off, Mordecai's roar of pain echoing through the ballroom. He hobbles in agony, lowering his head in submission, unable to meet my gaze.

I lean closer to the wounded dragon, my voice a hiss of malevolence. "Your punishment," I declare, "is to be forever bound to the girl you attempted to take with you. She shall carry your mark, and you shall remain tethered to her, a constant reminder of your disobedience."

If the broken claw isn't enough to show the rest of the Underworld that Mordecai fell from my grace, being tied to a soul will.

The dragon's eyes widen in fear and realization. Bound to someone else, forever linked to the one he tried to steal away from me, is a fate worse than any physical torment.

With a sense of finality, I step away, leaving him to nurse his wounds from the crash and his broken claw.

His betrayal couldn't have come at a better time. Not only did he open up the possibility of using him as Avira's guard, but it also ensures that the other dragons stay in line. If I thought Mordecai could take her to the surface, I would have let him. But I've tried to return her to where she belongs multiple times just to find out she's stuck here as much as I am. And I can't erase her memories again once they failed. Not if I want her ever to trust me.

FIFTEEN

Avira

When the door opens, I expect Otyx to stand in the door to tell me it's time for the second trial.

"I've heard what happened. Are you okay?" Netherius whispers, peeking into the chamber.

"You can't be in here," I say, covering the nightgown I found in a dresser to leave the feeling of the arena behind with a blanket.

"But I brought you something," he whispers, opening the door, and when my eyes fall on the scaly creature behind him, my heart jumps. Without thinking, I bolt out of bed and come to a screeching hold before the dragon.

"Did he hurt you?" I ask, pressing my face against its cold scales.

"Distance, mortal. Just because I let you ride on me doesn't mean I don't have boundaries," it says, and my heart jumps in relief, feeling its vibrating voice.

"I'm so glad you're okay." I take a step back and scan its body for injuries. When my eyes land on a broken claw, it moves his foot away and out of sight. "What happened?"

"I'd rather not talk about it," the dragon growls, looking past me into the room.

Adrenaline rushes through me. Not only did I survive the first trial, but so did the dragon. I whirl around to thank Netherius, and when I see the smile tugging on the corners of his mouth, I jump forward and wrap my arms around him.

"Thank you so much! I don't know how I can repay you," I say, pressing my cheek into his chest.

Carefully, he moves his arms around me and pets me on the back like he's never been hugged before and doesn't know what to do. "It wasn't my doing," he answers slowly. "But does that mean you're not mad at me anymore?"

Holding a grudge was never my strength. At least not since I started my new identity in Shadowmyre.

"I'm sorry for what I said. It wasn't fair," I say, pulling back, and when I look up, his dark eyes rest on my lips.

He's so close. Too close.

Scrambling backward, I cover as much of the see-through gown as possible before moving to the chair where I left the suit jacket I made for Lysander. Swiftly, I put it on and button it.

"I didn't mean to pry on you," Netherius says, diverting his eyes. "I just thought you could use some company."

"You're staying?" I ask, eyeing the dragon. "And Otyx allows that after what we've done?"

"For your protection," the dragon says, squeezing through the door into the room.

That doesn't sound right. After all, we tried to escape Shadowmyre together. So why would the God approve of bringing us back together? Doesn't he see me as a flight risk?

"There's more to the story. But it was a long day. We should rest," the dragon says, curling up beside the bed, taking over almost the entire room.

"And you? Are you going to keep us company?" I ask Netherius, my cheeks heating.

He cocks his head as he takes his surroundings in. "Do you want me to?"

"Yes," I answer, moving to my bed to sit down. "Don't get me wrong. I'm grateful Otyx didn't ban me to the Darklands for what I've done, but this room is so big and cold without all my belongings."

I'm used to my cramped room filled with colors, candlelight, and the voices of Ruby and Desiree. Just those few minutes alone in a chamber big enough to house at least ten souls has been an eye-opener. I don't want to be alone.

"Okay," he says, following me to the bed.

The silence between us is deafening. Occasionally, I hear the dragon breathe behind us as I study the Prince. He doesn't seem uncomfortable in this room. Of course not. How could he? He lives here.

"So what happened after I left?" I ask, trying to avoid the ache in my chest when my mind replays Gavin's death. As those words leave my lips, I realize I didn't see Netherius beside Otyx. "Wait. Where were you during Nekrojudex?"

He closes his eyes. "I'm not allowed to be in the same room as the God."

I swallow. How have I not noticed that before? I know from Ruby's stories that she had seen Otyx and the Prince at gatherings but never together.

"I thought you two are—"

"Inseparable because we rule the Underworld? We are. But we can't be in the same place simultaneously because if one of us gets harmed, the other can step in."

I wrinkle my nose. "Harmed? Isn't he indestructible? I mean, how can someone kill Death?"

Just the thought of trying to injure an immortal sounds laughable. Everyone knows the Gods are resistant to any type of attack.

"Even Death has a weakness," Netherius says, his eyes gleaming at me. "Eternal life might sound desirable, but when you're destined to spend it alone, you find out it's worse than any other cruel fate out there."

Without even trying, Netherius paints a picture of the God I could never put together on my own. He might be talking about himself, but he keeps referring to Otyx like he's the one suffering here.

"I was scared to meet you," I say, trying to break the fresh silence between us. "To be honest, I thought you would be just like him."

"And what would that be?"

"Cruel. Narcissistic. Power hungry." I shrug my shoulders. "I don't know because I've only met him twice. But after everything I've heard from other souls, it's easy to imagine the core values of the God. You, though," I say, shifting my weight. "You're different."

"Because I don't want you to see that side of me," he says, pushing his dark hair back, his eyes darkening.

"Then tell me: what do you do here? Everyone knows Otyx reigns over the Underworld, but what is your duty as the Prince?"

"That's what I'm asking myself sometimes, too," Netherius answers, laughing before he sits down beside me. "I see myself as the jester. While Otyx is busy collecting them and keeping them in line, I have the freedom to entertain them. Get to know them. They don't see me as a threat, knowing I'm just as doomed as they are."

My eyebrows draw together. "So, you are an entertainer?"

"Of sorts. What else am I supposed to do all day? I'm not allowed to cross paths with the God, and I'm trapped in the palace, the outskirts of Shadowmyre, and the Darklands. And believe me when I tell you, you don't want to spend time in the Darklands."

"Why?"

"Because those souls will never see redemption. They are so dark and twisted that even the God can't help them."

Help them? After sorting every soul into a specific sin, how is he supposed to help them? I'm missing something here.

Netherius' head shoots to the ceiling as if he hears something above us I can't.

"I have to go," he says, scrambling off the bed.

The urge to jump out of bed to follow him itches inside my muscles, but I keep pressing the blanket against me instead. "What's wrong?"

"Nothing. Don't worry about it," he says, smiling at me. "My job also entails that I need to help some souls out. And I'm needed right now."

As much as I want him to stay, I look over the edge of my bed and see the dragon huffing little smoke puffs out of its nostrils. I will be fine, at least until the second trial begins.

"Don't dream too hard about me," Netherius says, who's already grabbing the door.

"I haven't had a dream since I got here," I say.

I miss dreaming. I miss waking up, not knowing if I live in a delusion or reality. Those few seconds after waking from a dream are beautiful and short-lived. Somehow, I remember the feeling of trying to hold on to my dreams in my life before, but all of them are faded and unreadable.

"This place will change that," he assures me before closing the door behind him.

What is that supposed to mean?

I remove the jacket, throw it on the ground, and tuck myself into bed. There isn't much time until Otyx summons me for the next trial, and whatever it is, I might enjoy the last few hours I have in Shadowmyre before my soul ends up in the Darklands.

SIXTEEN

Avira

When the door creeps open, it's unusually dark. I'm used to my candlelit room or moonlight filtering through the heavy curtains, lighting up all the shiny tools and fabrics. But I'm not in my room anymore, and the low light is new.

"Are you awake?" a voice whispers from the door, and my eyes dart to the dragon beside my bed. The haze on my mind clears immediately when I find the spot empty. I'm alone. Where is the dragon?

"Who is it?" I ask, pulling the blanket higher and searching the room, hoping it had found a spot further away from me. No, I'm still alone.

"Netherius," the voice whispers, and my muscles tense. "Can I come in?"

"Is it time for the second trial?"

The silence that follows worries me. Did I oversleep? Has Nekrojudex continued without me?

A faint light flickers in the distance, giving me enough light to see more of my room. Scrambling out of bed, I lift the jacket off the ground and run to the dresser, where I find my neatly folded clothes.

"There's still time," he answers behind me. A shiver runs down my spine when I feel the warmth of his breath on my neck.

Slowly, I turn around. My breath hitches when I see water dripping off the ends of his curls onto his silken robe.

My mouth goes dry. "Then what are you doing here?"

"I need to do something I should have done the first time I laid eyes on you," he whispers, coming even closer.

My heart beats so fast it feels like I will faint any second. Without saying it aloud, I know what he wants. He made it clear from the first moment he pulled me onto the dance floor. Pressing my hands and butt against the dresser, I lean away from him.

"I can't," I whisper, watching his eyes darken as our bodies touch. I can feel his erection pressing against me through his thin robe, and my chest constricts.

As much as I want to lean into him, I'll give him the wrong sign, and he will continue. And even though I want to experience something I might have had in my life before, it can't be with the Prince of the Underworld. If I start something with him and my mother finds out, I'll earn the name I made up just to get out of Nekrojudex.

"I can't," I whisper again, closing my eyes to stop myself from wanting him.

Netherius takes a step back, giving me room to sort my thoughts. I knew what I was entertaining when I asked him to stay. Not only did I want to know more about him, but his presence soothes me.

But I never expected him to act on it. Not in the middle of the night when my fate is sealed.

My fate.

I'm already in Nekrojudex. Whatever I do now won't change the fact that I will end up in the Darklands. Everyone knows I won't become one of the Seven. And as much as it hurts to admit, I can't blend it out forever.

*But...*Mother of Lust introduced me as the Temptress when she announced my participation in the trials. So, what stops me from becoming the name everyone uses for me now?

I open my eyes and see Netherius taking another step back. "I couldn't help myself," he says, opening and closing his hands.

I've always been a good girl. The girl who helps others by offering to tailor their clothes and get them out of predicaments. The girl who was never tempted by another soul, even though lust is supposed to be my sin. The girl who spent ninety-seven years trying to figure out who she was. And I wanted nothing in return for what I believed in. Giving back to the other souls helped me stay sane.

But Netherius is offering me something. *Me.*

He's not asking for my help, and he's not here to push his sin on me. He's here because he wants *me*. And I want him.

Pushing myself off the dresser, I step close to him. "This can never leave this room," I say, ensuring that this thing between us isn't turning into a name I don't want to have.

"I promise," he growls, and before I can rethink my decision, his mouth is on mine.

Oh, Gods. He tastes delicious. My eyes roll back as our tongues collide.

Pressing myself against him, I lead him backward to the bed, not breaking our heated kisses. He wants this as much as I do. We come to an abrupt halt when his calves hit the bed frame, but I keep pressing until he falls onto the bed, pulling me with him.

"Slow down," he chuckles, brushing the hair out of my face. My insides heat when I see the smile curving his lips. He's handsome—so handsome that I almost forget to breathe.

But his words hit a sore spot. What if I've never done this before? What if, in my former life, I had no sexual contact with another soul? He could be my first, and I don't even know it.

"What's the matter?" he asks as I slide off him.

I shake my head. I'm overthinking this. Why does it matter if I was intimate with someone else before? Is that really going to hold me back?

"Nothing," I whisper, grabbing his collar to pull him onto me.

Netherius breaks our kiss. "We don't—"

"I want you," I cut him off, pressing my lips harder against his. The edges of my nightgown caress my thighs and stomach as he pushes it up, leaving me naked beneath. Frantically, I grab his robe to undress him, but before I can remove it, I feel his erection at my entrance. Pressing his weight on me, he uses his hand to slide into me, and I let out a moan when he inches in and out, stretching me.

It feels so good!

His eyes burn on my skin as he looks down at me, his nose wrinkling with every thrust. I can see the desire in his eyes—the fire in their darkness. Not knowing what to do with my hands, I reach out and grab his shoulder blades, and when my palms connect with his firm muscles moving under his robe, my eyes almost roll back.

"Faster," I whisper between ragged breaths, closing my eyes to take every inch. I can feel him move inside me. Whenever his hip connects with mine, I can feel his dick hitting a sensitive yet overly stimulated spot. Craning my head back, I concentrate on his movement. In shock, I open my eyes when I realize my nails are digging into his skin. Instead of finding a concerned look, I see him with closed eyes and a wicked smile playing on his lips.

He likes it. He likes the pain I'm inflicting with my fingers. Digging even deeper into the silken fabric, I feel his thrusts getting stronger and faster.

Wrapping my legs around his hips to give him total power over me, he takes the bait. The sounds of his feral moan almost push me over the edge as he moves on his knees and tilts my hips up, breaking my fingers' hold on him. The knowledge of him enjoying this as much as I do is too much. I search for something to hold on to as he drives into me repeatedly. Settling on digging my hands into the sheets, I arch my back more to direct his moving dick past my sweet spot.

Every thrust feels like a redemption to something I haven't felt before. Something warm claws inside me when he grabs my hips and slams into me. He's not gentle anymore. He's chasing this incredible feeling just as I am.

"You feel so good, my Fallen Angel," he groans.

My muscles tense at his words, and I feel the warmth seeping through my belly and back into my very center.

Losing control over my body, I let out moans of pleasure. As much as I try to keep them quiet, I can't. He thrusts harder into me until my muscles stop twitching and tensing, and when I can finally catch my breath, he comes to a standstill, yet he stays inside me. Why isn't he moving?

"You don't have to stop," I say, confusion clouding my voice.

"Watching you reach the high of your pleasure is everything I ever wanted," he says, pulling out to drop on the bed beside me. "Once the time comes, I will take what I need."

What does he need? I thought an orgasm was the goal for both parties. But somehow, he makes it sound like there's even more to it.

"Are you sure?" I ask, scooting closer to him to press my back and ass against him to change his mind.

"I will never get bored with seeing you being taken care of," he whispers, tracing my arm with his fingers. "Just give me that. Let me spoil you."

Nodding slowly, I stop pushing my backside into him. When his powerful arms wrap around me, I grab them, inhaling his scent deeply before my eyes become heavy.

SEVENTEEN

AVIRA

"**M**ortal. Mortal! Wake up!"

When my eyes flutter open, I'm startled when I look into red irises. Instantly, I'm wide awake, searching my surroundings past the dragon's eyeballs right before my face. My heart stumbles when I don't see another person sharing the bed.

Where is the Prince?

"Your mating cries are insufferable. Whatever you were dreaming of, it needs to stop," the dragon snarls, huffing little smoke balls out of its nostrils.

Excitement ripples through me as I recall the last images before the dragon woke me. Netherius. He was lying pressed against me on this bed.

"Where did he go?" I ask, knowing how stupid the grin on my face must look.

"Who?"

"The Prince?"

"You were alone in this chamber with me all night long."

My excitement is being replaced by shame. I imagined all of it. Of course, I did. Netherius warned me about the dreams in this palace. Was this his doing? Did he know I would encounter him in my sleep?

"You mortals are so peculiar," the dragon mumbles, turning in circles to find the perfect spot on the ground.

"Please stop calling me a mortal. I haven't been a mortal for almost a century. Avira will do just fine," I say, covering my face with the sheet to hide my humiliation.

"I guess this is the part where you want to know my name?" the dragon asks, and I lower the sheet to look at it.

"You have a name?"

What a stupid question.

"Doesn't everyone?" he growls, repositioning itself with its back to me. "I'm Mordecai and I'm a beaked dragon if you haven't figured that out yet. But I don't care what you call me."

"Mordecai," I say, testing his name.

"I'm already regretting my decision to give you my true name," he says, spitting smoke. "Anyway. Don't you have to get ready?"

My stomach turns as I think about what's coming my way. It doesn't matter what clothes I pick for the next trial. After all, I only survived the first because I tried to flee. This time, I won't get so lucky.

Crawling out of bed, I approach the closet close to the dresser. "Where did you—"

My mouth shuts, and my cheeks heat as the door opens and Netherius steps in.

Oh, no. What is he doing here?

"Ever heard of knocking?" I ask, submerging myself into the closet. I turn my face away so he can't read the shame covering it as I imagine all the ways his touch felt on my skin in my dream.

"You look rested," Netherius says, grinning at me. "Got a good night's sleep?"

Heat rushes into my face and core. If he knew… "It would have been better if I didn't know this would be my last day in Shadowmyre."

I can hear him stepping into my room without an invitation. "You're going to be just fine. Don't try to escape on a dragon's back again."

Pressing myself even further into the clothes on the hangers, I let out a quiet sigh. "How are you so sure?"

"I might not know the rules of the next trial because Otyx set up the rules for Nekrojudex hundreds of years ago, but those sins have nothing on you. You're the best contestant for it."

He wouldn't be saying that if he knew how hard I sinned last night in my dream.

"To take your mind off it for a while, I thought you could use some company," he adds, and I look over to Mordecai, who has moved his butt in my direction again.

"Not him," he says, shaking his head, and I follow his gaze to the door.

My heart stops when it flies open, revealing Ruby and Desiree.

"Girl. You're so lucky," Ruby bursts out as she marches in my direction. But her eyes are not on me but on the shining obsidian candle holders, a brush, and hairpins. "If I'd known this year's contestants get to spend their nights in the palace, I would have signed up for it." She lets out an ear-piercing scream. "And you have a freaking dragon? Are you kidding me?"

Pressing my lips into a thin line, I look at the Prince. "I hope the God doesn't mind missing a few of his belongings after I land in the Darklands," I smirk, knowing Ruby won't leave this place without a souvenir.

Desiree comes to a halt beside me, pulling out a dress. "Did you make those?" she asks, trickling through the two dozen dresses I'm hiding in.

Netherius clears his throat, and I peek through the fabrics to catch a glimpse of him. "I'm not needed here anymore," he says before exiting the room, leaving us alone.

As the door closes, I emerge from the dresses and hug my friends. It's childish trying to cover my body from the Prince because, in my mind, he has explored every inch of me already. But he doesn't know that. For him, nothing has happened between us yet. *No, not yet. There will never be a thing between us,* I tell myself, releasing Desiree.

"I'm so glad you're here," I say, fighting tears.

Desiree bites on the ends of her dark hair, a habit she does often when she has to leave her comfort zone. "I can't tell you how worried we were when your mother called your name. We watched you down there. Could you see us?"

"I couldn't see anything," I answer, biting my lip to stop my brain from replaying Gavin's death. I wouldn't be here if that dragon hadn't snapped him right out of the air as he tried to eliminate me.

"It was crazy. It looked like you guys were searching through a dark maze. And then Gavin tried to cut you down...and boom...a dragon shot out of nowhere, ending the first trial by chewing him up."

I tilt my head. "You didn't see what I did?" I ask, perplexed.

"You mean you tried to touch a dragon? Oh, everyone did. But just when we got to the good part, everything went dark."

That makes no sense. They should have seen me climb Mordecai. They should have watched us flying out of the arena. Unless...

"What's the next thing you remember?" I ask, watching Desiree push another strand of hair into her mouth.

"Otyx announced the contestants will be housed in the palace, and the next trial will be held today," she answers, making herself comfortable on my bed.

He did. He erased their memories. But why?

"What do you think is the next trial?" Desiree asks, fluffing up a pillow to get more comfortable.

"I'd rather not think about that," I answer, returning to the dresses.

"Come on. The least we can do is to get our champion dressed," Ruby says, skimming through the dresses. "But why dresses? Isn't that...unpractical?"

Desiree yawns. "The trials are not about fighting. They're simple mind games."

I turn to her. This entire time, I've relied on Ruby's information about Nekrojudex. Why haven't I considered asking someone who's constantly observing and just too comfortable to take part in anything? The souls belonging to the House of Sloth have a reputation for being overlooked and underestimated, and I did just that.

"What else do you know?" I ask, pulling out a red dress. Ruby takes it out of my hand and shoves it back into the closet before pulling out a white one.

Desiree shrugs her shoulders. "Not much. Only that every trial I've seen so far is more or less to test if you can withstand the temptation of your sin. All the failing contestants were eliminated because they caved."

I give Ruby a smirk. "You said there's fighting."

"Gavin attacked you," she says, throwing her hands in the air after putting the dress back.

"That's a choice he made, but not the essence of the trials," Desiree counters from the bed, her eyes shut already.

With this new information, Netherius' statement makes sense. I don't react to the sins if you exclude my thoughts of sleeping with a Prince.

"I won't wear white," I say, grabbing into the closet with closed eyes, and when I open them again, I hold on to the fabric of a thin, dark dress. When I pull it out and the light hits it, I notice it's the darkest shade of blue I've seen before.

"That's a little morbid," Ruby cuts in, trying to snatch it out of my hand.

"It's perfect," I whisper, holding it against my body. "So, are you going to help me or not?"

EIGHTEEN

Otyx

There's no reason for me to be this excited about Nekrojudex. It's a game. It's sheer entertainment, so my souls have something to do besides succumb to their sins. Even better, it keeps them on their toes to make a name for themselves just to join.

But the thought of seeing Avira again, so close to me, makes me forget to be disinterested in it.

Temptress.

That's the name she earned for herself if Isabella is right. And I can see why. I felt the temptation to touch her when I was called to collect her soul. Every nerve ending in my body told me to keep her close, save her, and make her mine. She does things no other soul has done to me, and she doesn't even know it. She's innocent, flawless, and kind.

That's precisely why I need to stay away from her. Whatever I'm making up in my head, it's only an illusion that will never become reality. Whatever I touch turns dark. And I can't do that to her.

I can't, and I won't.

Looking out at the souls taking their places around the arena disgusts me.

Are they here for her? Or are they just here to gawk at the souls who think they are better than the rest because they made it into Nekrojudex? Perhaps it's a bit of both.

As I announce the contestants, I clench my hands when I call out her name. She's not supposed to be there, but from all the remaining contestants, I know she will be the one standing at the end. I would bet my throne and title for it.

When I use my powers to bring the contestants into the arena, my heart stops when I see her pale complexion against the dark fabric she's wearing. Her blonde, braided hair falls over her shoulders with loose strains curling into her face.

Rage consumes me as I think about clawing everyone's eyes out to stop them from looking at her. Sharing her is something I never thought I had to do.

But the show must go on.

Looking down at the contestants, I watch the arena take the stage, forming six tables in a circle. I know this one, and I unclench my hands, knowing Avira won't have a problem this round.

"Today's trial is *Darkest Desire*. To be one of the Seven, you must show no matter what temptation or sin lingers around you, you will put your House first."

The crowd loses their mind as I lean back on my throne, and a smirk crosses my face as I watch her table stay empty.

NINETEEN

Avira

I need to figure out how the God does it—teleporting me from one room into the arena without even being present. A warning would have been nice, but I'm not in the position to ask for such luxury, especially since he pardoned me by not sending me to the Darklands early.

I hear the screams and applause above us as I again find myself in the enigmatic arena. Whatever is happening up there must have something to do with us down here.

As I stand within the circular confines of the arena, my senses sharpen, and I become acutely aware of my surroundings. The five other contestants stand at the edges of the arena, each one marked by a table. My gaze shifts, and my heart sinks when I realize there are six tables, one for each contestant—yet mine remains conspicuously empty.

Confusion grips me as I take hesitant steps toward my table, my feet stumbling over the uneven ground. I approach it with trepidation, my eyes scanning the surface for any sign of what awaits me.

To my bewilderment, the table appears bare, even under close inspection, devoid of sustenance or objects. Frustration wells up within me. What am I supposed to do?

A glance back at the other contestants deepens my unease. With a ravenous appetite, Olive sits at her table, devouring the sumptuous feast laid before her without hesitation. Plates piled high with food vanish before her insatiable hunger. It's fascinating and repelling at the same time.

My eyes wander over to the other tables. I can piece together what's going on when I notice gleaming treasures, a blanket and pillow, a blazing fire beside an ax, a beautiful silken gown, and a mirror.

He's playing with our desires.

I turn my attention back to my table, my frustration giving way to curiosity. As I peer closer, I realize that the surface isn't bare anymore. It's covered in a multitude of pictures, each one facedown and hidden from view.

My eyes come to rest on one turn-over picture. It shows a tiny babe, blonde hair whirling around her. She's neatly tucked into a white blanket, and her amber eyes look up at me.

A jolt of emotions courses through me. Is that...me?

With a sense of purpose, I reach out for the next picture to flip it over. Mid-air, I stop. No, something isn't right. Why would Otyx freely give us what we want?

My fingers tremble as I hover over the images that have to be snapshots of moments from my previous life, fragments of memories long buried beneath layers of the God's power.

I'm so close to seeing the faces of loved ones, places I've visited, and emotions I've once felt. Each picture could be a window into my past, a reminder of who I was and what I experienced before my journey into the Underworld.

"Don't touch it," I say, facing the other contestants. "He's testing us."

Ryder gives me a grunting noise as he grabs for the ax, weighing it in his hand while Olive keeps pushing food into her mouth. Why isn't she putting it down? Why does she keep eating even though I warned her?

In horror, I watch Olive's eyes widen as she keeps shoving food down her throat as if she can't bring herself to break away from it.

"Stop it," I whisper, looking away. "You have to stop this!" I repeat, looking up at the hole in the sky at Otyx. He's staring down at me, his fingers gripping the throne as if holding himself back.

Someone needs to do something. If Olive keeps eating like this, she will explode.

That's when I realize I made a crucial mistake. I haven't learned my lesson during the first trial. Turning my back on a man who just picked up a weapon is reckless. How could I forget that no one in this arena is safe from elimination? Frantically, I turn around, and when I see the gleaming steel raised high in the sky, my knees cave. The blade comes down on Ryder's arm in full force, and I whirl back around to cover my ears with my hands.

Unlike Gavin, he's not out to eliminate his other contestants. The sin he felt when grabbing the ax must have forced him to turn on himself.

"Don't look," Leo says, stepping beside me to shield me from the screams echoing through the arena. "It will be over soon."

I don't need to use my eyes to know how this round will end for Olive and Ryder. The smacking noises from Olive devouring food and the screams and ax hits from Ryder, hinting that he can't stop this violence now since he succumbed to his sin, forces bile up my throat.

"Someone needs to stop them," I yell, trying to stand up off the ground, but Leo presses his hand onto my collarbone to hold me in place.

"There's nothing we can do," he says as I look up to see his concerned face, half covered by his black and white hair. "Don't look."

I should fight him. I should slam him out of my way and reach for the ax before throwing all the food off the table. But the fear gripping me is suffocating. No matter how badly I want to break free, my muscles don't listen.

Do something, Otyx, I scream inside my head, trying to block out Ryder's scream.

They could have been eliminated after touching the objects on their tables, but no, Otyx revels in listening to their agony till the very end.

"We almost made it," Leo whispers through my fingers still enclosing my ears.

It only takes another minute before the air around me changes and the screams silence. When I open my eyes, I find myself in the room with Mordecai.

"How did it go?" he asks, jumping to his feet. "Must have been good if you're back."

I rush through the room and get to the washroom just in time to empty my stomach.

"That bad, huh?" Mordecai asks behind me as another wave of nausea washes over me.

Watching Ryder chop off his arm and Olive eating without restraint was horrible, but being so close to my past, just a fingertip away, was just as gut-wrenching. Everything I ever wanted was right there. Living in the Darklands, knowing who I am, would have been worth it. So why didn't I?

"If you want to talk, I'm here," Mordecai says, pulling his beak from the doorframe.

Silently, I wipe my mouth, stand up, and shuffle back into the room, where I find Mordecai beside the bed. Carefully, I step over his sharp claws to reach his belly. Without a word, I curl up on the ground beside him, pressing my back against his cool belly, and when his wing wraps around me, my tears flow.

TWENTY

Avira

Two trials in, and there are only four of us remaining. Four of us. How is that possible?

I need to talk to someone. Anyone.

"I wouldn't do that if I were you," Mordecai growls behind me, sharpening his claws on the floor.

"I can't stay here any longer. It's a prison."

"That keeps you safe."

"What if I don't want to be safe? I can't go back into that arena. I'll be eliminated anyway if he allows me to see my past again. Nothing is holding me back from uncovering my past."

Mordecai stills for a moment. "Then why didn't you?"

That's the question I've been asking myself while I cried myself to sleep under his wing.

"I don't know," I say, pulling on my hair. "It was right there. I was so close." I reach out my fingers as if I could still grab the images through my mind.

"And yet, something kept you from giving in."

Rubbing my forehead, I pace through the room. "That's the problem. There's nothing that stopped me. It was just me...and—"

"We have been at it for hours. How about you lie down and close your eyes or whatever you mortals do to fall asleep?"

"I'm rested," I bark, picking up speed. "I'm sorry. That was uncalled for. I didn't mean to snap at you."

"It's fine. I mean, your teeth can't snap hard enough to do any damage to my scales. Do whatever you must do to get that anger out."

Anger.

For years, I haven't felt this enraged. Correction. The last two days, I've felt more anger than in my ninety-seven years in Shadowmyre. But that's precisely why Ryder isn't here anymore. Wrath caused him to chop his arm off. What if Ruby is right? What if I have another sin I react to, and I've been ignoring it?

I stop to inhale deeply before exhaling.

I can't lose my cool now.

Looking over at the dragon, I cock my head. "Did you just make a joke?" I ask, recalling his snapping comment.

The fine hair on my neck reacts to his claw scratching over the stone ground as he looks up at me. "Whatever I need to tell you to stop you from pacing, say it, and I will do it."

Slowly, I relax my face and throw myself onto the bed. "Why would a God choose to reign over a kingdom under the surface?" I ask, trying to get my mind off the last trial.

It was a rhetorical question, but when Mordecai answers, I stiffen.

"To have a kingdom on the surface, he needs mortals to worship him."

I sit up straight. "That's it?" It makes sense. Why haven't I thought of that before? Could it be this simple?

"Yes, and impossible to achieve as the God of the Underworld. Who wants to pray to a God responsible for collecting souls just to damn them for eternity?"

Fair point.

My thoughts wander to the outskirts. "But he tried to reach the surface, didn't he?" I ask, rubbing my knuckles. "That's why the other Gods decided to ban Emberix."

Mordecai growls. "He didn't try. He actually made it; whatever happened up there was horrific. He only walked the surface for a day, and when he returned, he had an army of souls behind him."

My mouth goes dry. "He went up there to kill mortals?"

"What else did you expect him to do? I remember the day like it was yesterday. It was the busiest we dragons have been in a long time. You know how hard it is to keep a new soul in the Darklands? Now imagine thousands are overrunning you." He lets out a smoke puff, blowing it in my direction. "And it's happening again."

Fear claws at my chest. "What do you mean?"

"The day before Nekrojudex started, we got a ton of new souls delivered."

I've noticed it, too. When I went to find fabric to make something for Lysander, the room was cramped with armor. Back then, I thought nothing of it.

Could that be the reason Netherius had to leave yesterday? Is there something more significant going on than he wants me to know?

Another thought swirls through my mind as I try to piece all the information together. Otyx is up to something. But what could it be? He can't reach the surface again, not without Emberix.

But maybe he doesn't need her.

"What are you really doing here?" I ask, stiffening.

Mordecai eyes me curiously. "What do you mean?"

"I saw Otyx slamming into you in the arena. He was mad. It almost looked like he wanted to kill you. So why would he allow you to stay in my room?"

Mordecai huffs and rolls his eyes. "To protect you. What else should I be doing here?"

No. That can't be it.

"I don't need protection," I answer, balling my hands into fists.

"Are you sure? You looked pretty pathetic when you wept under my wing."

"I was decompressing." I gasp. "Are you going to use that against me?"

"You cried like a mortal baby. I still have snot on my scales to prove it." Mordecai lifts his wing to show me the spot, and I laugh. He's not trying to be funny, but he is.

He lowers his wing and stares at me. "Look at me, Avira. It's not bad to feel emotions. Letting them out is good as long as it doesn't consume you. You're emotional. So, what? Amongst all the sin-ridden souls, be you. Be vulnerable. Let your emotions guide you."

Another tear threatens to cross my cheek, but I blink it away. "You really suck in cheering someone up," I say, my voice laced with emotions. "But I know you're trying your best." I reach for him in a desperate attempt to connect to someone living. Someone who isn't dead or trying to harm me.

"I'm not a pet," he growls, moving his head away, but his neck moves closer to me as he turns.

"Amongst all the other dragons out there, you're my favorite," I say, closing in on him. This time, Mordecai doesn't move away. I welcome the cold sensation beneath my fingers as I touch his scales.

"Because I'm the only one you know," he grumbles, leaning into me. "If another dragon finds out I let a mortal touch me, I will deny it."

I laugh. "No one will ever know," I whisper, reaching out my other hand to trace the patterns on his neck.

TWENTY-ONE

Otyx

I almost lost her. I saw the longing in her eyes. She wanted to flip over those images, and I could have done nothing to stop her.

Did I really believe she didn't have a dark desire? After years of watching her, I gathered enough information to know her better than her *friends*. I know everything about her because she is my darkest desire.

But she can never find out what forced her countdown to start. It will break her heart.

For the Underworld's sake, it broke mine, and she doesn't even know. No one should ever experience what she went through.

Just the memory of it makes anger rise inside me. She deserved so much better. Better than what the mortal world offered and better than what I could give her in Shadowmyre. That's precisely why I couldn't let her go to Zorus, knowing she would've remembered her life. It would have darkened her and her spirit.

Fuck. She would be better off if she could just stop digging for the past. If she could just trust me, I would make sure nothing ever happens to her.

I shake my head.

It's too late. I already let her down by letting her take part in Nekrojudex. I can't even interfere with a game I created, and I don't have to mention that she's stuck down here because of me.

She'll never trust me. Whatever fantasies flood my brain whenever I look at her will never become a reality. She'll never get to know me. She'll never know I tried to save her soul from an even worse fate.

I close my eyes.

That's another lie. She will know what I've done. Once she becomes one of the Seven—and I know she will—her memories will return to her. Then, her hate will change her. It will consume her until nothing is left of the Avira I know.

TWENTY-TWO

Avira

A knock on the door forces me to jump out of bed. A fluttering feeling ripples through my belly. It has to be Netherius. I haven't seen him all day.

Rushing to the door, I rip it open, and my smile vanishes when I see my mother.

"I'm so glad you're alright," she says, pushing herself into my room. "Trust me when I tell you, I made a mistake. He put me on the spot, and when I saw you, I reacted."

That's not the soul I expected to find on my doorstep, and it's too late to reverse it.

"So, you selected me because I looked at you?" I ask, closing the door behind her.

"I knew when I saw you that you could be one of us. One of the Seven. That's what every soul wants. You get your own House, and you can do whatever you want," she answers, eyeing Mordecai.

Her eyebrows lowered to form a 'V'. Disapproving of the company I keep, she ignores him and strolls to a mirror I've been avoiding to look at her reflection.

Reluctantly, I follow her. "That's maybe what everyone else desires, but not me. I liked what I had. I never wanted more."

Isabella huffs, throwing her hands in the air. "You're saying that now, but wait until you see yourself at the top of the soul chain."

That's precisely what I can't picture. It's laughable imagining me as one of the Seven. Besides that, I don't want a Head of a House position. The thought of being surrounded by souls who only want to get close to me for their own benefit is nauseating.

"What if I want your House?" I ask with a forced smile.

Her face gets even paler than usual. She opens her mouth, but I cut her off.

"I'm just kidding."

But am I? Until now, I haven't even thought about what to do when I have to pick a House. None of them speak to me. If I'm the last contestant standing, I *have* to pick one. Envy and pride seem the least cruel from what I've seen. Leo even tried to shield me from Ryder's screams in the arena, which is atypical for a soul belonging to pride. Gods, it's abnormal for any soul down here.

"Don't worry. We both know I won't come out as the champion," I say, waving my hand.

Isabella's eyes meet mine through the reflection. "That's where you're wrong. I know you will."

I hold my breath. She's the second person telling me that. But how do they know? I almost caved during the last trial. What if Nekrojudex sensed my hesitation? What if it uses my weak spot—my desire to discover my past—against me again?

"Whatever happens, remember, I didn't mean to sacrifice you. I picked you because I believe in you. You're my most-liked soul. All I want is the best for you."

I bite my lip as I take her words in. While I always knew I was her favorite, even if she can't say it aloud, she scares me with her outspokenness. I can't shake the feeling that something is wrong. Mother of Lust doesn't apologize. Technically, it wasn't an apology, but it was as close to one as anyone can get from her.

"I know you meant well," I say, watching her pick her nails. "But have you found out what happened to Lysander?"

Isabella's eyes narrow. "To be honest, for a moment, I thought you had something to do with his disappearance or your so-called *friends*. I thought you might have changed your mind about Nekrojudex and didn't know how to ask to join. From what I've heard, he must be in hiding. Some wandering souls also whispered about the Prince seeking you out again after the Nekro-Ball. Did you—"

My cheeks heat at her implication, and my heart races as I think about his naked body. *Darn, Avira. It was just a dream. Everything you saw was just your imagination. Handsome and well-built, but still a delusion.*

"He just came to check on me," I answer, walking to the washroom. "And if you don't mind, I must prepare for the next trial."

"But, Avira. To make a name for yourself, you need to seduce him," my mother says, following me.

How can I? If I entertain the thought of getting closer to Netherius any longer, I will fall for him. Perhaps it might even be too late if my dream was an indicator. The only thing worse than falling for the Prince of the Underworld would be to fall for the God himself.

But can eternally doomed souls fall in love, or do they just act out of lust? Maybe Otyx was right, and I belong in the House of Lust after all.

My body aches as I inspect the hole left in the ground in the center of the room filled with water. Carefully, I dip my toe into it; to my surprise, it's warm. "You already announced to the entire Underworld that I'm Temptress. I don't need to do anything. Your words have way more weight than any action I will ever do. And the souls already saw me dancing with Netherius. That alone seems to have spread through Shadowmyre like a fire."

TWENTY-THREE

Avira

It didn't take long after my mother left for someone else to knock on my door. I knew better than to hope for Netherius, and yet, my heart ached when an unfamiliar soul asked me to follow her.

Is he ignoring me? Have I upset him? Even worse, does he know about my dream? Has he figured out why I couldn't face him when he brought Ruby and Desiree to my room?

"Where are we going?" I ask the soul, staring at the dark curls that bounce with each step as I follow her. I'm met with silence as she leads me down corridor after corridor into the opulent ballroom bathed in perpetual twilight.

My heart hammers in my chest as I step over the threshold, remembering the feel of Netherius' touch. Back then, I couldn't wait to get away from him. Now, I would give everything to be in the same room as him again.

Darn it. I'm in too deep. This wasn't supposed to happen. Stop thinking about him.

My mind reels back to reality when I see the other contestants spread out in the vast room. I'm not surprised to find Leo sitting on the throne, stretching out his long legs while Ava's eyes throw daggers at him. On the other hand, Sawyer looks like he's ready to nap, and I giggle because he reminds me so much of Desiree.

"What's so funny?" Ava snarls at me, turning her icy gaze toward me as she shows off her perfect figure in another tight dress.

"Leave her alone. She saved our asses during the last trial," Leo cuts in, rising off the throne while adjusting the cufflinks of his black suit.

"I would've never touched that dress," Ava growls, smirking at him. "Green isn't my color."

"Is that so?" Sawyer asks from a corner. "Then why did your eyes light up when you saw it?"

She rolls her eyes. "Because I haven't seen another color than black, white, or gray in ages. Not everyone is as lucky as the Daughter of Lust." I cringe under her stare. "What makes her so special, anyway?"

I straighten my shoulder as Ava strolls toward me, taking in the saffron-colored dress I picked after my mother left.

"Your face is turning green," Leo laughs, coming to a halt beside her. "It suits you."

Ava throws her gray curls over her shoulder and stomps away.

"Now we're even," Leo whispers, circling me. "But seriously. Why are you still colorful?"

I'm regretting choosing such a vibrant color, knowing that no one else, not even the God, can touch something colorful without draining its pigments.

"It's because she hasn't committed to a sin yet," Sawyer whispers from the corner, and when I look past Leo, I see him sitting on the ground, leaning against the wall. "Am I right?"

I don't know, but his explanation makes much more sense than anything I came up with.

"I—"

"It's none of your concern, soul," a dark voice vibrates through the room. My eyes dart to the throne. There, seated upon the imposing obsidian throne, is the God of the Underworld.

When did he get here?

The atmosphere in the ballroom is palpably charged as an unsettling silence falls over the contestants. His form is shrouded in darkness, his eyes like twin voids that bear into my soul. His presence is suffocating, an aura of ancient power that smothers all hope. But somehow, it's also comforting.

"I've had other matters to attend to," the God declared, his voice a chilling undercurrent of authority like rumbling thunder in the distance. "But now, I can finally turn my attention to my final four contestants."

I receive uncertain glances from the others. They act like it's their first time standing before Otyx without a crowd. But it's not just that. They look scared as if he will shred their souls into a million pieces if they look up to him.

However, the God of the Underworld offers no words of praise or encouragement to ease their discomfort. Instead, he speaks with an air of disdain, his tone condescending as he addresses us.

"Three of your fellow contestants have already fallen," he announces, his words a stark reminder of the unforgiving nature of the trials. The boundaries of reality and illusion are fluid in Shadowmyre, where the test lies in discerning truth from deception. "But you, the final four, remain. Don't think of yourself as special. You're merely survivors, nothing more."

The other contestants listen in silence as I try to wrap my head around the fact that he acts so differently than I remember him. I also recall Mordecai's words. Whatever Otyx's plan was, he must have fulfilled it, and now he has all the time in the world to dedicate himself to us.

Oh, Gods, he's looking straight at me. I never thought I would pass the first trial. Yet here I am, awaiting number three.

With an imperious gesture, the God rises from his throne and descends to the floor of the ballroom, his presence commanding the attention of all.

He continues, his voice laced with cruel amusement as he leans back. "The next trial will test your willpower even further," he declares. "You have endured two challenges, but now you will face a trial of the mind. You will be confronted with illusions, deceptions, and temptations that seek to cloud your judgment."

I see Sawyer's wary glance as he makes his way close to us. I just stand there in rigid silence, unable to take my eyes off Otyx.

The God's gaze washes over us once more before a smirk forms on his lips. "One more thing," he says, his voice taking on a sinister edge as he lifts a finger. "Tomorrow's trial will be your last. Only one of you will stand before me once the full-blood moon lunar eclipse ends."

A collective unease sweeps through us as I absorb the God's words, and my eyes widen when the information settles in. It's impossible. Tomorrow can't be our last day. I'm not ready.

With a flick of his hand, Otyx gestures toward a portal that materializes on the far side of the ballroom. It radiates an ominous aura, an invitation to a test with promise and peril. We have no choice but to heed the God's command.

As I approach the portal after the others, each step filled with a sense of foreboding, the God's following words echo in my mind. "Remember," he warns, his voice trailing after me like a chilling refrain, "in the Underworld, the true test is not merely survival but the strength of your spirit. The trials will reveal who you truly are."

With that, I cross the threshold, disappearing into the unknown depths of the Underworld, back to a place I know all too well: the arena.

TWENTY-FOUR

Otyx

I watch them depart with an inscrutable expression, my eyes filled with a dark amusement that leaves no doubt—this realm will continue to test the mettle of those who dare to venture within its shadowy embrace. That's how it has always been. Keeping them on their toes prevents them from falling victim to excruciating boredom.

Isn't that the reason I was created? A God bored enough to create his own insignificant planet to watch other souls suffer? I don't want to imagine what eternally doomed souls can do once bored.

But when I watch Avira step through the portal, my mask slips. I have to warn her. It's just her and me in this room, alone.

"Remember, in the Underworld, the true test is not merely survival but the strength of your spirit. The trials will reveal who you truly are."

I want to say more, but Nekrojudex's hold on me prevents it. I could reach her in time to pull her into my arms to stop her. If I could end Nekrojudex, I would. If I could take her and bring her back to the surface where she belongs, I wouldn't hesitate.

How am I so fucking powerless? It's my kingdom! There must be something I can do to stop this. But I know there isn't. I plugged every loophole when I created Nekrojudex to ensure that every selected contestant has to take part in the trials, no questions asked.

My only option is to contact Zorus to explain that I wrongfully took a soul that didn't belong to me. It has never been done before, and he warned me that once a soul enters either of our kingdoms, it's there to stay. For the Underworld's sake, he's the King of the Gods, the creator of this planet. There must be something he can do.

But I'm too selfish. I can't let her go. Never!

Breathing in deeply, I follow her into the portal. She's even stronger than I thought. Even though Nekrojudex found her weakness—her past—Avira will beat the others. And I will be there when her memories crush her. I will be there when the realization hits that the actual monster isn't me or this place, but her past.

TWENTY-FIVE

Avira

I exhale sharply when my feet land on the dark, slick arena ground. No matter what happens next, I know everything will be over tomorrow. If I make it to the fourth trial, I will never have to enter the arena again.

Closing my eyes, I inhale the musky air before glancing at the two towering doors before me, each one radiating an aura of profound significance. The choices before me are stark, and the consequences of my decision weigh heavily on my mind.

The first door shows blurred scenes from my past that have long been lost to me. I know it's my past because I can see the flowing blonde hair amidst the white background and hear a woman call my name. Behind this door lies the chance to relive those cherished moments, to rekindle the emotions and experiences that have been buried in the depths of my mind for far too long.

My gut wrenches when I force myself to look at the second door to my right. It shows a dark altar with an object. Without ever seeing the object, I know the second choice leads to a chamber where a mythical artifact awaits. It possesses the power to heal and restore the Underworld itself, mending the fractures and soothing the eternal suffering of its souls. Choosing this path would be an act of selflessness, a sacrifice even.

Without taking a minute to think about it, I steer to the left. I told myself I would pick my memories if they were presented to me again. This is my chance to regain the part of me I've been longing for. It will also ensure that I get out of Nekrojudex before I end up as the champion and have to pick a House.

Remember, in the Underworld, the true test is not merely survival but the strength of your spirit. The trials will reveal who you truly are.

I won't listen to the God. He deceived me once, and I won't fall for it again.

The coldness of the doorknob cuts into my skin as I curl my hand around it. I can feel my past pulling me into the room without opening it. It's warm and weightless, like a summer breeze brushing the hair out of my face.

Taking another deep breath, I step away from the door.

It's not right. Knowing the other choice offers a chance to heal Shadowmyre, how can I pick my past? Maybe the artifact is strong enough to bring colors back to the Underworld. Perhaps it can aid the suffering souls in easing their torment and bring hope to their existence. It offers a chance to be a beacon of change in this shadowy realm.

My heart wrestles with the decision. I want to grasp the elusive memories that slipped through my fingers when I arrived. My identity remains a puzzle I yearn to solve.

But as my gaze shifts to the door on the right, the image of the suffering souls of Ruby and Desiree and the possibility of making a meaningful difference tug at my conscience. I know that my action could have a profound impact on the Underworld, where countless souls endure an eternity of anguish.

With a deep breath, I make my choice. I turn away from the door before me and step toward the other. By choosing this path, I won't only be aiding others but also embarking on a journey of self-discovery that will reveal my character's true essence.

Isn't that what I want?

I can't change the past, so why am I clinging to it? What good will come from knowing the life I can't return to? I can't help the mortals on the surface, but I can change the realm surrounding me with this artifact. Hope is a precious rarity in the Underworld, and I can deliver it to them.

Bolting through the door, I come to a screeching halt before another set. Straightening my shoulders, I inspect my options. The door to my left has three words carved into it: *Who am I?* The other says *Shadowmyre's secret*.

Without seeing the other sides, I can feel a hidden chamber filled with ancient tomes and scrolls that hold vital knowledge about the workings of the Underworld behind the second door. Choosing to delve into these texts could provide invaluable insights to help maintain the Underworld's equilibrium. But it also means forsaking the opportunity to regain personal memories—again.

Biting my lip, I step through the second door without giving my past another glance, just to find myself in front of two more choices.

Your heart's desire is written on the first, while the other shows a staircase deep into the heart of Shadowmyre.

My heart stops. Why did the door change? I was set on bursting through the next one and the next one, walking away from my past. But that's not what's waiting behind the first door. Somehow, it feels like my deepest desire has shifted. But if it's not my former life, what is it?

Fleeting images of Netherius cloud my mind. The way he took my hand on the dancefloor. The smirk he gave me when I asked him to stay. The way his skin felt on mine in my dream.

Oh, Gods. By steering my heart and mind away from the only thing I've desired since I got to Shadowmyre, I opened the door to let something, or rather someone else, in—Netherius.

Stepping closer to the second door, I reach my fingers out to get a feeling. This doorway leads to a realm where I can make a selfless sacrifice that will significantly benefit the Underworld, reinforcing its foundations and ensuring its continued existence.

Stumbling back, I take the doors in.

If I choose the first one, does that mean I get what my heart desires? Does that mean Netherius will be mine, even if he doesn't feel the same about me?

Holding my breath, I choose my door, and when I open it, I find myself back in my room.

TWENTY-SIX

Avira

"How did it—"

"Don't," I snap, rushing past Mordecai to get to the washroom. Splashing cold water into my face, I try to wash away the choices I made in the arena.

I still don't regret choosing the Underworld over my memories. I've been chasing after something that won't change my situation in the slightest bit.

But the last choice I made hurt. It hurts so much that my muscles tense thinking about it.

"There's someone here for you," Mordecai says, his voice filled with compassion. "Should I send him away?"

Him?

My heart pounds in my throat. Netherius is here. I know he wasn't there to see me choose a door, but it doesn't take long for news to travel through the Underworld.

He probably knows...No, maybe he even feels what I've done.

"Let him in," I answer, drying my face with my sleeve.

"You sure?"

"Yes," I say, mentally preparing myself for what's coming next.

When I enter the chamber, I see the smile forming on Netherius' lips. His dark eyes sparkle as he takes me in, his gaze wandering over every inch of my dress.

"Who was eliminated?" I ask, my voice shaking.

"Pride. Leo chose the door to Shadowmyre's throne."

My stomach turns. I liked him. Maybe we would have become friends if Nekrojudex hadn't made us eliminate each other. But that seems insignificant after what I've done. This isn't the reason why he's visiting me.

"You know, don't you?" I ask, lowering my head.

Netherius' brows draw together. "Your last choice?"

"I can explain," I say, rushing forward so he can see the honesty in my eyes. "I wanted to pick you. I really did. But to keep the Underworld spinning, I had to take the other door."

Netherius' smile slips.

Oh no. He didn't know. He didn't know that I selected the door that led me away from him. The door that could have given me his heart.

"Your heart's desire is *me*?" he asks, stepping back.

I open my mouth to say something, but the embarrassment cursing through my veins makes me shut it again.

In the heat of the moment, my choices still burning in my mind, I forgot I might be the only one who saw what lay behind those doors. How could he know that my heart's desire changed after I kept skipping my memories?

But there's no taking it back. I said what I said, and he heard it.

"It's silly, I know. I mean, I barely know you. We just met a few days ago. We—"

Netherius crosses the room in two strides and presses his finger against my lips. "You don't have to explain yourself," he says, his eyes flickering, "because you know I feel the same about you."

My heart jumps into my throat, and when he lifts his finger, I move even closer and kiss him. This kiss is nothing like the one we shared in my dream. It's desperate and deep. It's as if my soul is set on fire, in a good way.

I moan as his hands drive through my hair before he slightly pulls on it.

And as fast as it began, it ends.

"I need to go," he says, pulling back. Deep creases form between his brows as he stumbles backward, shaking his head.

My body goes stiff. "Did I do something wrong?"

I watch him back away from me even further. "No. There's just something I need to do."

Right now? At this moment? Somehow, my dream played it so differently in my head, and the thought of him changing his mind mid-kiss fractures a part of my heart. Did he just confess that he feels something for me? Or was it just another cruel game my mind played on me?

"Just give me a little bit of time," he says before rushing out the door.

That's it? That's how our first *real* kiss comes to an end? He has to go because there's something more important? I mean, I get it. I chose the Underworld over him not even an hour ago. But *seriously*?

Breathing heavily, I look over at Mordecai, who pretends to sleep.

"I know you're awake. You blow little smoke bubbles when you sleep," I say, and he opens his eyes. "What should I do? I can't let him leave like this."

Mordecai looks at me in horror, shrugging his wings.

If I had more time, I would let the Prince go until he's ready to face me again. But I'm a contestant. Tomorrow isn't promised. If he doesn't make it back in time for the next trial, I might never see him again because I will be moved to the Darklands.

I storm out the door, ignoring Mordecai, who's trying to press himself through the frame to hold me back. Just down the corridor, I can see Netherius. He's shaking his head as he opens the last door on the same floor just as I shout his name. But he doesn't react. Or maybe he heard me, and he's just ignoring me.

Panic settles in my bones as I run down the corridor, bursting into the same door I saw him enter, and when my face collides with a massive, undressed chest, my knees buckle.

"I'm sorry," I whisper, taking a step back into the corridor, and when I look up, my chest constricts. "I must have picked the wrong door," I whisper to Otyx as he builds himself up before me. Frantically, I look left and right. No. This is the door. I know it.

He growls as I take another step back, trying to decipher where I went wrong. The silence between us is so unbearable that I press out the only question that comes to mind. "Is Netherius in there?"

The God of the Underworld's eyes flash with surprise at my question. "No," he says firmly before stepping into the hallway and closing it.

"I saw him. He went into this room," I answer, repeating Netherius' last movements repeatedly in my head.

He crosses his arms. "You're mistaken."

"I saw him. He was right here and then...what did you do to him?" I ask, finding my voice. As I try to look past him, Otyx covers the entire door with his shadowy form. He's hiding something.

"I know he's in there. Let me go to him. Please?"

But Otyx doesn't budge. Instead, he unfurls his wings, taking up even more space. "You won't find him in there," he says again.

That's when my fear that something happened to Netherius turns into anger. Within a heartbeat, I'm wedged between the God's hips and wings to reach for the doorknob behind him. Startled, Otyx grunts as we fall into the chamber's opening door. Scrambling to my feet, I feel the God's hands curl around my ankle, and I kick him off.

"Where is he?" I yell, storming from the vast chamber into the washroom and back. "Where did he go?"

When I look into the God's void eyes, my stomach drops. "Tell me!"

"He had to go," Otyx says, standing up, and another wave of anger threatens to consume me.

"So, he was here?"

The God nods, and I notice his shoulders drooping just an inch. Something still doesn't seem right. He can't just vanish. And then there's the rule that the Prince and God can never be in the same room. Unless...

I take a step back.

If Otyx wanted to, he could have used his claw-like nails to injure me when he held my ankle. But he didn't.

I take another step.

Even though I tried to escape on Mordecai's back during the first trial, the God didn't punish me. Instead, Mordecai showed up on my doorstep with Netherius.

Another step.

No one has ever seen Otyx and Netherius in the same room because...

I shake my head over and over again. "No. Please tell me it's not what I think it is," I say as bile rises in my throat.

"I don't know what you're referring to," Otyx's answer, but the way he looks at me, I know he's lying.

"It's *you*," I croak, touching my lips, still burning from Netherius' kiss. "All this time, it was *you!*"

Flashbacks hit me like bricks. Netherius taking my hand in the ballroom. His disappearance right before Otyx took the stage. Netherius telling me about Emberix. My body almost hitting the ground while Otyx dove after me. Netherius showing up with Mordecai right after the God forced me to stay in his palace.

"You...you're Netherius, too," I stammer, clutching my chest.

"Don't be foolish," the God says, shaking his head. "His room is right beside us."

No. It's not. And we both know it.

"I know what I saw. He went into this room," I say, pointing at him. "Tell me the truth."

My heart aches when I wait for the words I already know.

"I need to go," he says, walking away.

"But I'm not done with you," I yell after him as he leaves me behind. Running after him to make up for my short legs, I watch as he steps onto a balcony on the other side of the corridor. He turns around to face me. "I promise I will explain everything to you when I return," he says, expanding his wings, and that's the last thing I hear before he throws himself over the railing and takes off to the clouds.

No, he won't. Because by the time he comes back, I will be gone.

TWENTY-SEVEN

Otyx

Fuck. She wasn't supposed to find out about me. How could I've been so reckless? I always double-check my surroundings before changing.

But her kiss, the way her hair felt when I grabbed it, and the moan that escaped her lips when I tried to pull her closer sent me over the edge.

Right then, the call I received to claim incoming souls was untimely. But if I would have stayed, I would have done things to her I can't take back. Even worse, things that would have broken her if she had found out who Netherius really was.

It was cruel to use the Prince to get close to her. I refrained from using that illusion for that exact reason. But when she stormed into my dressing chamber just seconds before the Nekro-Ball began, it opened a door for me. It's like fate brought us together. Introducing myself just to talk to her, to hear how she was doing out of her mouth instead of just watching her, was freeing.

Yet, I should have stayed away from her when she revisited the outskirts. I knew the risks and ignored them because she was not like the other souls, and being close to her was like seeing the natural sun again and not the fake one I'd created down here.

I thought I had more time to keep it going. But for what outcome? That she falls head over heels for a soul that doesn't even exist? For a person I made up to get closer to the souls I claimed?

I should have known that it would never work out. Love isn't meant for Gods and neither for doomed souls. She's not immortal like me. Eventually, her time will run out, and I will lose her for good.

That doesn't change that she'll never forgive me for what I've done.

Maybe Zorus knew about the destructive nature of portraying another soul when he gave us Gods the ability to shapeshift. Perhaps he knew that once the mortals find out that we could be anyone in their inner circle, without even knowing, it would create chaos.

I wish I didn't have to leave her this way, but my duty is calling. Like her, when she picked the Underworld over her heart's desire, I have to do the same. If I'm not there to collect the souls, they will storm into the Underworld, confused and with their memories intact.

I will explain everything to her once I'm done with the war happening on the surface. I must.

TWENTY-EIGHT

Avira

How could I be this foolish? How could I think for a minute that the Underworld is safe? Sins, deception, and lies are the fuel that keeps this place going.

Still, it hurts so much knowing that the God himself was playing with me. For the Gods' sake, I was falling for him.

Nausea ripples through me as I recall all the moments with Netherius. He was so honest, so kind, so imperfectly perfect. How can this all be a lie?

Why me? From all the souls he could have tortured, why me? I did nothing to anger him. Well, besides my attempt to reach the surface. But he entered the picture before I decided to escape. I asked Netherius so many questions, and the entire time, he answered like Otyx was not him.

Let's just say that the God and I share a special connection. He might be the immortal collecting the souls, but I'm the one keeping them in line.

A special connection. A connection so deep that they are one and the same.

He was here for a moment. I think he finally took the time to approach the soul he has been dying to meet again.

My mouth goes dry. He told me. Netherius told me that Otyx reached out to a soul he longed for. Back then, I felt revolted but thought nothing of it. Now, I know. He was talking about me. Everything he told me wasn't a lie; he was just stretching the truth. How could I have known the Gods could change their shape?

In less than a minute, I'm back in the chamber Otyx imprisoned me in. When I slam the door, Mordecai jumps to his feet, showing his razor-sharp teeth inside his beak until he realizes it's me.

"Back so soon?" he asks, curling his tail around himself.

"Did you know?" I scream, pointing my finger at him.

"You figured it out," he whispers, closing his eyes. "Our oath prevents us from talking about the God's intentions. I wanted to tell you, but I could do nothing."

"He has been playing with me," I press out, anger burning so hot inside me I might catch fire. "Do you remember my promise? I told you I would get you out of here. Let's go."

Mordecai flares his wings. "We can't go. Not even the Darklands will be enough for our punishment if he catches us."

A laugh erupts in my throat. "He won't do anything to us," I answer, grabbing the suit I made for Lysander to throw it on.

"You're too confident," Mordecai says, turning his head away from me. "He already bonded me to you. Do you know what that does to a dragon? You're my weakness, and I must keep you safe to survive."

I whip my head around to stare at him. "That's why he brought you to me? Your punishment is to be tied to me?"

He growls. "Bonded to you. If something happens to you, I'll have to live with the consequences."

Everything is making sense. I wondered why Otyx allowed Mordecai to stay in my chamber. Until now, I knew I had some weight on the God but didn't know how much.

"We're leaving," I say, pushing my arms through the jacket sleeves.

"But if he hurts you? What if he punishes you? Or me?"

"I promise you, I'll keep you safe. But right now, we need to go before he comes back."

Frantically, I push my feet into my boots, grab a pillow, and rip the bedding off the mattress. "Lay down," I command. Knotting the blanket and thin sheet together, I climb onto Mordecai's leg to position the pillow right above his shoulder blades in front of his wings.

"What are you doing?" Mordecai asks as I step down.

I ignore him. "Stand up." I throw the blanket over his back until I see it dangling on the other side of his leg. "If I was in my chamber, I could have tailored a saddle for you, but this has to be sufficient for now."

Fastening the blanket and sheet under his belly, I pull on the fabric to ensure it's tight.

"Your scales are sharp," I say, inspecting my makeshift saddle from a distance. "I promise I will remove it once we're on the surface."

Growling to himself, Mordecai takes a step forward, testing his wings, and I have to shield my face from the objects flying through the room.

"Very well," he says, kneeling again so I can hop on. It's the same gesture he did before we took off in the arena.

"Not here. There's a balcony just outside this door we can use," I tell him, opening the massive front door to let him through.

Peaking my head into the corridor, I look around. No one. It's now or never.

"Fast," I hush, stepping into the corridor.

When Mordecai was delivered to my room, I didn't notice the problems he must have had getting through. Watching him pulling in his limbs and squeezing through the rocky frame hurts. How did he get into the room?

"I got it," he breathes, almost dislocating his left wing.

"Hurry," I whisper as distant footsteps ring in my ears. "Someone is coming."

Mordecai inhales sharply. Holding his breath, he pushes his entire weight forward, and I startle when half of the wall breaks loose, falling to the ground before me.

So much for a silent exit.

The footsteps in the distance turn from a walk into a run.

"Can you move any slower?" I ask as Mordecai carefully steps over the broken stone pieces. "The damage is done. No need to walk on eggshells."

My heart stops as I see a woman round the corner. I know her. She's the soul that brought me to the ballroom to meet the other contestants. I wait for her to scream at us, and when nothing happens, I bolt to the balcony, Mordecai following close behind.

"I jump, and you catch me!" I scream over my shoulder.

The second the balcony comes into view, I regret my decision. What if Mordecai misses me? What if I fall to the ground? Falling this far, I'm guessing ten stories, can't be pretty.

But I don't have time to second guess. If something happens to me, Mordecai will feel it. Therefore, he won't let me hit the ground.

I hurdle over the balcony's railing, and once I fall over the edge, my life in Shadowmyre flashes before my eyes.

Amidst the endless twilight of the Underworld, I plummet through the air in free fall, the sensation of weightlessness engulfing me. The world around me spins in shadows and enigma, and I'm suspended in the vast emptiness, my heart racing with a potent mixture of exhilaration and uncertainty.

As I descend, my eyes search the obsidian abyss below, where the ground remains obscured by layers of darkness. The inky void stretches infinitely, its depths unfathomable. I've made a choice, a leap of faith, and now I await my guardian of the Underworld to fulfill our unspoken pact.

In that suspended moment, the air whispers secrets only the Underworld can hold. My senses are heightened, my every heartbeat echoing in my ears.

Escaping the palace is one thing. But what am I going to do once I'm free? Do we try to reach the surface's crust again? Do I ask someone for help? But who? If the way out of the Underworld was easy, souls would seep out like flies.

Then, just as the abyss threatens to consume me, a powerful presence approaches from below. It's Mordecai, soaring up to meet me in a breathtaking display of grace and power. His scales glisten with an otherworldly luminescence, casting a radiant glow amidst the shadows. The dragon's wings unfurl with the precision of a masterful pilot, catching the currents of the Underworld with a resounding whoosh.

In that surreal moment, I descend slowly as I feel the dragon's presence drawing near. And then it happens—a union of trust and destiny. The dragon's outstretched wings envelop me, its scales brushing against me with a cool and comforting touch. I'm cradled within his powerful embrace, my fall arrested by the might of the creature's wings.

I cling to Mordecai's back, settling my butt on the pillow, my heart pounding in tandem with the rhythm of our flight.

We did it! We got out!

I gaze around the Underworld's inscrutable beauty unfolding before my eyes. The shifting shadows reveal the buildings souls are sorted in, seven palaces on every star point, and secrets and wonders beyond my imagination. The sensation of flight carries an exhilarating sense of liberation.

With each beat of his wings, I feel a plan form in my head. I'm not getting out of here alone. If I find a way out, I'll take Ruby and Desiree with me.

"Catch her," Mordecai growls, and I furrow my brows, not understanding what he's referring to.

When I look up, I watch a woman—no, not any woman, *the woman* from the corridor—hurdle through the air. Her mouth is wide open, but she's silent. My eyes widen, and without overthinking it, I reach my hands out to meet her.

"What is she doing here?" I scream as my fingers grasp her shoulders, pulling her into a sitting position before me.

"She held onto my tail. I thought I could shake her off, but she wouldn't let go."

Great. If trying to outrun Otyx's grasp wasn't enough, now I pulled another soul into my mess.

"What do you want?" I ask, clinging to her.

She turns her head around to meet my eyes, and I expect her to answer me. Instead, she throws her hands up and starts waving them around with no rhyme or reason.

"I don't understand," I say, shaking my head. "Just tell me."

Mordecai shifts his weight under us. "She's deaf."

Realization hits me. That's why she didn't answer my question when she led me to the ballroom. She never heard it. And those bizarre hand movements, she's trying to communicate with me.

"What are we supposed to do with her?" Mordecai asks. "And where are we going?"

It's too late to turn around and bring her back to the palace. After what Mordecai did, the entire Underworld must know what we've done. That's another reason we can't return.

"She's going with us," I say, wrapping my arms around her to hold her in place. I envisioned her to fight back, but she just clings to his scales, holding on for dear life. "Are you sure she can't hear us? If she's deaf, why did she fasten her pace when the wall crumbled?"

"Vibration," Mordecai answers, stating the obvious. "In the Darklands, vibrations are the only thing to help you navigate the tunnel systems. It's pitch black down there."

Feeling ashamed for not knowing how it feels to hear nothing, I press her tighter against me, hoping she can feel my apology. How could I've been this ignorant? I should have noticed it.

"I need a direction," Mordecai says, and I frantically search the ground below us. "Down there. That's my room. Can you bring us close?"

She signs something, but I can't make it out.

"I don't understand," I say, shaking my head.

She points at me, Mordecai, and herself, then makes wing motions with her fingers before she points at the clouds.

"You want to come with us?" I ask slowly, pronouncing every word carefully as I repeat her motions.

She nods furiously.

"Ok," I say, turning around to unlock my door with the key around my neck. Inside, I grab two dark cloaks I made, a stack of blank paper, and a piece of charcoal. Pressing everything into her hands beside a piece of paper and the charcoal, I write as fast as possible.

What's your name?

She looks at me, then at the paper.

"Please tell me you know how to read," I whisper, taking the clothes back before handing her my question. She grabs for it, and before I can say anything more, she answers.

Maeve.

There are so many things I want to ask her, but when I see Mordecai shifting his weight outside to hide in the shadows, I know it's time to go.

"Come with me," I say to Maeve, watching her eyes follow my lips. She nods. I wish I could learn to speak to her, using her hand motions. But if we wait any longer, Otyx could be back.

Pointing at Mordecai, I whisper. "Go."

She looks at me with wide eyes. "I need to get my friends," I add, and with another nod, Maeve runs to the dragon while I spin on my heels and burst into Ruby's room.

Thanking the Gods when I see her pale skin and white hair, I let out a sigh.

"What are you doing here?" she asks, her brows drawn together.

"I don't have time to explain. I need you to trust me," I answer, grabbing her arm to pull her with me. But as my fingers curl around her, my eyes wander over the objects surrounding her.

It has been years since I set foot in her room. I was so used to her seeking me out that I never had to visit her. But when I see the overflowing piles of stolen goods, my eyes widen.

"I can explain," she stammers, following my gaze. "I never—"

"They're colorful," I say, looking at all the missing things I knew she took from my room. "How is that possible?"

"It's only *your* things," Ruby says, grabbing a pair of boots off the ground. "See. I grabbed those outside someone else's room, thinking I might be able to restore them. But I couldn't."

She holds the boots in my direction. "Touch them."

Reluctantly, I drive my finger over the worn-out material, and my heart rate quickens when the black turns into a navy blue under my touch.

"It's you. Every piece of yours inside this room doesn't fade because of you. I thought by collecting them, I would get a fraction of mortality back—just a fraction of hope. But I was wrong. I should've never taken from you." Tears dwell in Ruby's eyes, and I grab her cheeks, pulling her face closer to me.

"I'm not mad," I say, tears stinging in my eyes. "But next time, just ask."

My eyes catch on the sparkling scissors beside her bed. The object catapults me back to the outskirts when Netherius stepped out of the darkness. Or should I say Otyx?

"What about Desiree?" Ruby croaks out, ripping me out of my thoughts.

"I got it," I whisper, grabbing her hand once more to lead her out of her room, leaving all my former belongings behind.

TWENTY-NINE

Otyx

I haven't set foot in the mortal world during a war in such a long time; I forgot how sweet the screams of mortal souls sound. Hidden in the shadows, cloaked by my darkness, I watch the young Queen crumble under her dead father's blistering stare. He must be my best creation yet.

Giving him the power to resurrect the dead is just one of the few perks of sending him to terrorize the kingdom that keeps on taking. If it wasn't enough that one kingdom can harbor magic to use whenever they please, they also rely on it to heal themselves.

Cheating death always comes at a price.

While they see nothing wrong with manipulating their bodies to outlive their expiration date, I know better.

I've devised many ways to collect souls surpassing their mortal time. During the last war, I personally took it upon myself to lure the Crymzon Army onto a battlefield. But since Crymzon is ruled by the new Queen, I didn't have time to address the matter because of Avira. No, that's wrong. I could have made the time, but I didn't want to. Instead, I created a threat that the young Queen couldn't resist—her father.

Watching him terrorize his still-breathing daughter wasn't easy. He knows he can't touch her. It's not her time yet. But that rule doesn't apply to anyone I've marked to be collected.

Still, when I'm called to the battlefield, I'm surprised to see Eternitie's Army doing a better job cutting down Crymzonians than my creations.

Closing my eyes, I can feel the internal clocks of the soldiers ticking. I know who will fall, when, and where, and I chuckle when I feel Eternitie's ruler on my list. The irony of seeing him marching against another kingdom just to end up dying is bittersweet. He would have lived for another few hundred years if he hadn't gone up against the Crymzon Queen.

Minutes turn into hours as I wait for the battlefield to clear until I can rush to the waiting souls to claim them.

I count them carefully to ensure I've collected enough Crymzonians to even the scales, and to my surprise, it is. Reaching the last soul, I hold my hands out to present the seven glowing orbs resting on my palms. Immediately, the woman's mind grabs the red one, and the second she reaches it, her physical color drains, and she vaporizes.

Exhaling, I look over the battlefield at the carnage left behind. I have to thank King Citeus for finishing my job. Without him, it would have taken me another battle or two to be done with Crymzon. But he won't remember anything when I see him again.

Finally, I can return to Shadowmyre to talk to Avira. Nothing stands in my way to focus solely on her, save for the occasional soul dying of natural causes. It's time to call all the souls Keres resurrected to lure the Queen out back and let them rest until, maybe someday, they're needed again. But for now, they have served their purpose.

THIRTY

Avira

Finding Desiree seems more complicated than expected. Neither Ruby nor I know where her room is.

"Explain it to me again. You're trying to get out of the Underworld because you don't want to become one of the Seven?" Ruby asks behind me as Mordecai flies for a third time over the buildings in case Desiree spots us. "And you tamed the dragon that was resting in your room when you got there and found a non-verbal friend to help you escape?"

What I told her isn't too far from the truth. I don't want to join the Seven, and while *taming* is a harsh word for trying to touch Mordecai in the arena, and Maeve isn't a friend yet, I can't tell her the truth. If we get caught, I can plead for Ruby's innocence. And even though telling her about Otyx and Netherius is on the tip of my tongue, that's another detail I must keep to myself for now.

"That sums it up," I answer, scanning the ground once more. "But if she doesn't show up soon, we must leave her behind."

Ruby clears her throat. "Are you sure Desiree wants to join us?" she asks behind me. "I mean, I want her to come. But she's happy in the Underworld."

Ringing with myself, I have to accept that Ruby is right. As much as I want to take Desiree to the surface, convincing her to leave everything she has in Shadowmyre behind will be challenging.

Swallowing my emotions, I point at the palace in the far east. "Bring us to the House of Lust," I say to Mordecai, scanning our surroundings again.

Souls scream as Mordecai descends from the twilight-lit skies and lands before a foreboding black palace. The structure looms like a sentinel of shadows, its spires and turrets casting long, sinuous silhouettes that stretch across the ashen ground.

As we dismount, a sense of unease settles over me. I brought my old and new friends here with a singular purpose—to seek answers from the one individual who might hold the key to escaping the Underworld: my mother.

Together, we approach the grand entrance of the palace, its obsidian doors towering above us like a portal into an abyss. My heart is heavy as I push open the massive doors. The echoes of our footsteps reverberate through the cavernous corridors as we venture deeper into the palace's depths.

Finally, we reach a chamber shrouded in shadows, and there, upon a throne carved from ebony, sits Mother of Lust. Her visage is ashen and ethereal, her eyes reflecting the lustful ways she can lure men to their knees. She regards me with sadness, as if she knows the weight of the questions that I will ask.

"Mother," I begin, my voice trembling, "is there a way to escape Shadowmyre?"

My mother's gaze remains steady as she gestures for me to come closer while she descends from her throne. "Come, my child," she breathes, her voice like a mournful sigh. "Let me show you."

Excitement bubbles up inside me. Why haven't I asked her sooner? Maybe the key is to ask the right questions to get answers. After all, it worked on Mordecai.

I step forward, my heart pounding with hope. Isabella reaches out a spectral hand, and as I touch it, an inexplicable power surges through me. At first, it's a sensation of warmth, a golden light that envelops me. But then, to my horror, a golden cage materializes around me, its tangled bars locking me in place.

Ruby cries out in alarm, and Mordecai, sensing my distress, lunges forward, claws extended as he tries to scratch through the impenetrable metal. His claws dig deep, but each time he retracts them, the metal strengthens again.

The cacophony of desperation fills the chamber as my mother looks at me sorrowfully. "I'm sorry, my dear," she whispers, her voice laden with an ancient sadness. "There is no escape from the Underworld, for its bonds are unbreakable. You're bound to this realm, just as I am, and everyone else. I already lost one soul. I can't lose another. You need to finish Nekrojudex."

How could I be so stupid? In my haste, I ignored every warning about Isabella. Tears well in my eyes as I realize the cruel truth of my mother's words. The golden cage is an inescapable reminder of my fate, and the despair in my heart is mirrored in the eyes of my friend and dragon, even Maeve.

She didn't select me because she thought I would win. She chose me as a sacrifice. Isabella knew I would never question her decision. I wanted to. Instead, I believed her. Every lie she told me. I gobbled it down like Olive devoured the food.

"What did you do to Lysander?" I ask, lifting my palm to stop Mordecai from further draining his energy. With sad eyes, he stops and backs away.

"That coward fled. No one knows where he is. I tried to find him in time to throw him into the arena, but it was like the Darklands swallowed him. I never meant you any harm. When I called your name, a piece of my heart chipped away. But I needed someone spectacular to show the strength of my House. And I needed someone who wouldn't claim my spot among the Seven."

"Why are you telling me all of this? There's still a chance I could win Nekrojudex."

Isabella chuckles. "Even if you do and decide to challenge me, I'm not worried about it. Has anyone ever told you the last phase of Nekrojudex?"

I try to recall everything I know about it. "Once the trials are over with one remaining contestant, that champion can pick the House it wants to rule over."

"No. The champion picks a House and has to win the seat by combat."

Cold sweat forms on my skin. I search for Ruby's eyes, but she stares at the ground, avoiding eye contact.

So Ruby was right, after all. There might not be any fighting during the trials, but Nekrojudex will end with bloodshed.

"I'm sorry it had to come to this," Isabella says, stepping closer to the cage. "You know what breaks my heart? Even now, you don't feel angry after knowing everything I just told you. It's not in your nature to hold grudges or to press conflict on others."

She's right. I should feel something after her betrayal. I should try to reach her through the bars and scratch her eyes out. I should still be mad at the God for using another man to get close to me.

But I'm not.

I understand their reasoning. Mother of Lust is a good Head of Lust. She loves what she does, and there are no complaints under her rule.

And Otyx...I don't know how I would have reacted if he had asked for my hand instead of Netherius. Without using a less intimidating persona, I would have never met the gentle side of the God.

But that's why I need to get away from here.

"I wish there was another way," Isabella says, wiping a tear off my cheek.

With a heavy heart, I know I'm trapped within the realm I've sought to escape. The palace's dark corridors now seem to stretch on forever, and the answer I desired is nothing more than an elusive mirage in the eternal twilight of the Underworld.

THIRTY-ONE

Otyx

Anger boils inside me when I land on the balcony and am greeted by souls trying to repair a wall I know was intact when I left.

"What happened?" I bark as the realization sets in that it's Avira's room.

"There was a dragon," someone whispers, sweeping wall pieces off the floor.

"What about the girl? Is she still in there?"

The souls exchange confused glances, and I'm so close to banning every single one of them to the Darklands. "Where did it go?"

They point back to the balcony, and my heart stops.

She made it out. But I already told her that Mordecai can't reach the surface. Did she try it again? Did the knowledge about me send her over the edge?

Grinding my teeth, I step out onto the balcony, looking down on my territory. If I was Avira, where would I go? Scanning the sky, I don't see any wings that could indicate Mordecai is carrying her away—that traitor. I told him to keep Avira safe.

Then it hits me. She would never leave without her friends. Not because she can't live without them, but because it's the right thing to do. No one down here does the right thing. Selfishness paired with at least one sin is the motto in the Underworld.

But not for Avira.

Opening up a portal, I imagine her room in Shadowmyre, and with one step, I'm there. As I look around, nothing seems out of place. If she was here, she took nothing with her.

I burst through the door onto the street, shadows snarling around me.

"God of the Underworld," a voice says beside me, and when I turn my head to face the soul, it crumbles to the ground, pressing its forehead against the rough ground.

"Where's the girl?" I growl, my anger rising like brewing lava.

"House of Lust," the soul answers, its voice muffled.

Opening another portal, I'm gone before it can lift its head to look at me and step into Mother of Lust's palace.

At first, I believed myself alone in the throne room draped in obsidian shadows, its atmosphere heavy with an uncommon stillness.

But then, my eyes fall upon something that sends another surge of anger through me. A golden cage stands in the room's heart, bathed in an ethereal glow. Within its radiant confines, a blonde woman sits, her form pressed against the bars with a look of desolation etched upon her face.

As I draw closer, my gaze locks with Avira. Her eyes, once filled with fire, now hold a glimmer of defiance. She meets me with a steady, unwavering stare, as if challenging the very essence of my being would set her free.

With three steps, I reach the cage. The golden bars gleam in the dim light, casting patterns of radiance and shadow upon the chamber's floor.

"What has she done to you?" I whisper, grabbing the bars.

"She just reminded me that I'm trapped here," she whispers, undaunted.

My rage intensifies at her words. Trapped? That's how she feels about my kingdom?

With a wave of my hand, I dismantle the cage to release her. Her lips curve into a semblance of a smile, as if she knows something I don't. "You see, Otyx," she says, her voice tinged with a hint of irony, "not everything in the Underworld is as it seems. Even a God may find himself trapped by the very mysteries that dwell within."

My anger giving way to a gnawing curiosity, I contemplate the woman before me, and my heart aches. I've broken her. Everything I did to protect her ended up failing. I should have stayed away from her. I should have let her be. She was doing just fine without me meddling with her head.

As our eyes meet again, I know that this unexpected captivity has changed her. Her defiance is a spark of rebellion within a realm of shadows, and I, begrudgingly, find myself intrigued by it.

"You were never supposed to find out," I say, lowering my head.

"And then what? Would you have kept playing with me? With my feelings? At what point would you have had enough?" There's no edge to her voice. No anger. No sadness.

Feeling Nekrojudex pulling on my essence, I shake my head. Not now. I need time to talk to her. But if I don't react within this instance, it will pull me to the arena unwillingly.

"We have to go," I say through clenched teeth. "But after—"

"Don't," she cuts in, holding her hand out. "I've had enough. Your secret is safe with me, but I can't continue like this."

I practically hear her spirit break. Her once gleaming and beautiful soul is now draining like everyone else's.

I've betrayed her trust. Mother of Lust threw her in a cage. And Mordecai seems to have cut his ties to her because I can't see him anywhere.

"I'll get you out of here. Out of Shadowmyre." I swallow hard. "After this trial."

Snapping my fingers, I'm once more dragged to the throne above the arena, and when I look down, I see Avira, her blonde hair now dull and white, her jacket dark and drained of color.

Knowing how much she longed for her past, I thought the trials might break her. But I never expected to be the one responsible for her surrender.

Yet, right now, I can't help her. Nekrojudex demands my presence. It will pull me back if I try to break loose.

Summoning all my courage, I address the crowd. "And the next trial—"

My mouth fills with acid as I watch a river forming beneath me in the arena. All eyes are directed at me.

Fuck!

I need to go down there and take her away. Maybe I can lure one contestant into the river before she ever sets foot into the water. Anything is better than what's brewing down there.

A cough brings me back to reality.

"The next trial is *the River of memory*," I announce and watch in horror as Avira steps to the river's edge, not even minding that this will be her end.

THIRTY-TWO

Avira

Is this how it feels to be hopeless? This emptiness, cursing through every fiber of my body, numbs everything I felt before. It's like I'm drowning, yet totally aware that I do nothing to change it.

While I might not escape the Underworld, I couldn't deny my friends that chance. Forcing Mordecai to take Ruby and Maeve to the surface without me was heartbreaking, but I couldn't be selfish. I hope they made it.

Within the depths of the arena, I stand at the precipice of a broad, churning river. The water before me appears as an inky liquid, its surface agitated and frothing with an unearthly intensity. I don't even look for the other contestants. It doesn't matter where they are or what we must do, because I won't compete this time.

Without hesitation or a flicker of hope kindling deep within me, I take my first step into the freezing water, knowing this is the last trial. The chill seeps into my bones, sending shivers coursing through my body. Yet, I press on, each step more painful than the previous. Once I reach the middle, I'll let the current take me into the Darklands.

As I venture further into the river, the icy waters seem to carry me away, not physically, but through the corridors of my memories. Scenes from my past, long buried in the recesses of my mind, rush forth like a torrent. I see fleeting glimpses of laughter, tears, and moments that have shaped my identity but have been shrouded in the shadows of the Underworld.

The memories flow through me like a cascading waterfall, an overwhelming flood of emotions and experiences. I feel myself becoming one with my history, the past weaving seamlessly with the present as I fight to maintain my footing in the frigid waters.

I don't know what the task is. If Otyx wants me to reject my memories again to show my selflessness, he's wrong. Instead, I accept every heartbreaking moment of it.

I see my mother and my father. I see where I grew up and how I was treated in the mortal world. A gasp escapes me. I had everything. *Everything*! Until, just like Isabella, my mother chose something, or rather someone, over me.

As I lift my head to the throne, I see Otyx's concerned eyes. Oh, he knows what is happening. He knows that every shred of the past he sucked out of me is rushing back. I can see in his gaze that he tried to shield me from this.

But I had enough. The longing to become part of the Darklands vanishes with each wave.

As I look past him, the celestial canvas of the Underworld's arena unfolds in a breathtaking display. A full-blood moon lunar eclipse is underway, the moon's radiant red glow dimming as it passes through the shadow of the realm. It's a celestial dance that mirrors my struggle—a battle against the encroaching darkness to unearth the light of my forgotten past.

With every step, my resolve solidifies. I never wanted to win Nekrojudex. I never intended to come this far. But with every wave of memories washing over me, I feel the fire in my heart ignite.

I was always like this. Forgiving. Finding happiness where others can't. Putting other people's needs before mine and sacrificing myself for the greater good.

But not anymore.

I push forward, fighting against the current that seeks to pull me under. This river of memories can't deter me.

As I finally reach the other side of the river, my legs trembling and my breaths ragged, I feel my past settling. The eclipse above me has passed, and the moon's luminous presence emerges again, casting its radiant light upon me like a benediction.

Above me, I can hear the crowd roar to life. The numbness I felt when I stepped into the freezing water is replaced by nothing other than rage.

How could she do this to me? How could my mother trade my soul for someone else's? I was her flesh and blood, yet I wasn't enough.

Slowly, I search the river for the other contestants, and when I don't find them, I lift my head to the crowd.

The moonlight vanishes for a moment as Otyx flies down into the arena. As he touches down gracefully before me, the atmosphere pulses with anticipation. The other souls watch in hushed reverence, knowing that this encounter holds profound significance.

Looking around, I notice I'm the only one who reached the other side of the water. That's it. I'm the final contestant. I made it. The trial wasn't to reject my past. It was to accept and survive it.

His eyes are inscrutable, posing the question that has lingered in my heart since Isabella called my name. "Which House do you choose?" he inquires, his eyes searching every inch of my body.

I, however, don't yield to the God's expectations with haste. Instead, I consider my options. "I need time to think," I reply, my voice unwavering, "I don't want to decide now."

A murmur ripples through the arena, a collective inhalation of breath as all eyes turn toward me.

The God, unaccustomed to hesitation, regards me with curiosity and authority. "You must choose," he declares, his words brooking no further delay.

Instead of bowing to Otyx's command, I chuckle softly. "Must I?" I retort, my eyes sparkling with a glimmer of mischief.

The arena falls into a hushed silence as all await the God's reaction to my brazen challenge. The choice of a House is a sacred rite in the Underworld, and defying the God's command is unprecedented.

Otyx, his patience tested, regards me with an unyielding gaze. "I'm Otyx, the God of the Underworld," he declares, his voice carrying the weight of eons to keep the spectacle going for the souls, "and your defiance won't be tolerated."

"Then, my God," I reply, my tone unwavering, "if you desire an answer, you shall have to force it from me."

My defiance hangs in the air like a cyclone, challenging the foundations of Otyx's order. The arena remains shrouded in an uneasy stillness as the God and I lock in a standoff of wills.

I won't jump anymore because he tells me to. I won't let him push me around anymore. If he wants me to pick one of the Seven to fight, he must respect my decision that I need time.

"Very well," he says, gazing up to face his souls. "Our final contestant will announce her House at tomorrow's ball."

He snaps his fingers before I can ask questions, and I'm teleported back into the palace.

THIRTY-THREE

Avira

"Why did you take me?" I ask Otyx as my feet touch the ground in the room I woke up after the first trial. "You could have rejected my mother's offer. Instead, you took my soul to resurrect him."

"That's not entirely true," he says, his shoulders slumping. "I'm sorry, Avira. This is the part where I usually congratulate the champion for passing all trials. For a minute, when your color began to drain, I thought I lost you."

"I don't need your cheers. Just tell me the truth. I saw my mother offering my soul to you so you can bring my father back. Why did you do it?"

"There's more to it than your mother's proposal."

"Then tell me what it is!" I scream, looking up at him.

"When Queen Caecilia called me to Starstrand, your father was already dead. It was his time to go; even Zorus doesn't meddle with life or death." He pauses as if recalling standing before the deceased King. "Your mother didn't think clearly when she offered your soul to me. She thought she could bring your father back and save you after his return."

"What happened?"

"I told her that there's no return once a soul is claimed. Still, she didn't budge. So I did the only thing I could think of."

So many emotions flood through me. I don't know what to feel. My mother chose my father over me. The woman meant to protect me exchanged my soul to bring her King back.

"I cheated," he says, and confusion clouds my mind. "Instead of ripping your soul out of you, I traded another one for yours. I couldn't kill you when I saw you. You were vibrant, full of life, and incredibly naïve even to consider taking you with me to save an unsavable man. You have to know a resurrected soul is fractured and facile. Queen Caecilia didn't get her love back. Instead, she had to accept that she offered her only daughter for a broken soul. Within a day, I felt your father's expiration again. This time, your mother freed his soul because she realized he would never be the same."

I should feel sad. Not only did my mother lose her daughter, she lost the love of her life twice. But the only thing I feel is pity.

"So, what about me? Why didn't you tell me sooner?"

"How could I? Once you grabbed my hand, all your memories vanished. When I brought you down here, you seemed content. I tried to bring you back to the surface. But when I failed, I erased the attempt. That's why I panicked when I saw you on Mordecai's back. Again, playing the bad guy was easier than letting you experience defeat."

My mind swirls as I listen to him. "How can I trust you? You deceived my mother. When you accepted her proposal, you knew my father would never be the same. And don't get me started on Netherius. So how am I supposed to know if this isn't just another game of yours?"

"Because everything I ever told you is true. You're indeed the most beautiful soul I've ever seen. I've indeed been dying to talk to you. It's true that I bonded Mordecai to you, not because I thought you needed protection, but because you needed a companion who's equally obsessed with you as I am. Whatever you want me to do to prove myself, I will do it."

My heart pounds in my chest. Every fiber in my body tells me not to trust the God of the Underworld. But my heart tells me otherwise.

He gave me clues about my past.

Fallen Angel.

Princess.

Perhaps I could have made the connection if I had listened to him.

"What about Emberix? Was she your dragon?"

Hurt clouds his face. "She was. And she was magnificent."

I want to ask more about her, but I've been interrogating him since we entered this room. As much as it hurts me to relive my past and hear what my mother has done, I can feel the hurt I caused the God.

Clenching my teeth, I shake my head. Otyx shouldn't take up this much space in my head. He did this to me. Why does it hurt knowing that he's in pain? He's the one who betrayed me. He's the one that kept me away from my family, my life. Yet, all I want is to ease his discomfort.

"The third trial," I say, and his eyes meet mine. "I didn't know what my heart's desire was. I thought it was my memories, but when I stood before the last set of doors, I could feel it. At that time, I knew for certain that my heart longed for a part of you. Netherius might be a persona you slipped into to get to know me, but he's still you."

I take a step closer.

"I know it's foolish to believe that a God could fall for a soul, but whatever I saw in your eyes every time you looked at me, it felt so real," I say, lowering my eyes.

"Because it was," he answers, lifting my chin with his finger to meet my gaze. "The way I approached you was wrong, but I couldn't find another way to get closer to you than using Netherius."

I need to steer away from this topic. As much as I want to hear it, this thing between us can't continue. Whatever I feel for him, I need to swallow it down. With time, the pain will ease. With time, he will forget about me.

"So, what now?" I ask, moving away from him to break his spell on me. "Until the ball, I need to decide which one of the Seven I want to fight?"

Taken aback by my abrupt topic change, he swallows, and his eyes darken. "There's no other way around it. The rules state that the champion needs to announce a House after victory."

"It sounds like there's no deadline. *After victory* could mean today or in a hundred years."

Otyx considers my words for a moment. "I've never run into the problem that the last contestant doesn't want to choose," he says, tilting his head.

"What if I don't choose? What if I hold off picking a House until the next Nekrojudex comes around?"

"I don't think—"

"At least let me try," I plead. "I promise I won't flee again."

"We both know it's impossible anyway," he answers, shaking his head.

"Then I promise I'll never undermine you again," I say, bowing before him.

"Stop that," he says, stepping towards me, but I back away. He sighs. "Okay. But if Nekrojudex demands a name, you have to give one. And if it doesn't, I'll take you to the surface after the ball, as promised."

Nodding my head, I watch as his feet walk out of my view towards the door. As he opens it, my heart screams to call him back, to not let him leave this room. But it's for the better; we both know it.

THIRTY-FOUR

Avira

I wonder where Mordecai, Ruby, and Maeve are now. Were they able to see me win Nekrojudex? Or did they go through with the plan to find a loophole to get out of Shadowmyre and the Underworld?

The time is ticking. In a few minutes, I need to leave my room for the ball. All eyes will be on me, the victor of this year's trials.

But since I set foot in Shadowmyre, it has been the same. As the only soul with a colorful aura, I stick out. My light might have dimmed momentarily in the arena, but it's now even brighter than ever when I look at my reflection.

I pace restlessly in front of the closet. The night is illuminated with the weight of a choice resting upon me. There's still the possibility that I have to choose a House tonight.

My fingers dance over the rich, delicate fibers of the gowns, each tailored to perfection. I consider the silken blues and velvety purples, their beauty matched only by the myriad of colors in the moonlit sky. Yet, none of them feels suitable for this event.

Until my gaze falls upon it—the gown tucked away, hidden in a shadowed closet corner. The gown is fashioned from the purest silk, a fabric that has been meticulously selected to embody the opulence and sophistication befitting a grand ball. Its sheen is like liquid gold, a luminous quality that catches the light and scatters it in a dazzling display. The silk's surface is smooth and sumptuous to the touch, evidence of the impeccable quality of the material.

The golden hue of the silk isn't merely a color; it's a radiant glow that emanates from within the fabric itself. It shimmers like sunlight, reflecting off rippling water and casting a warm aura around its wearer.

The gown is adorned with intricate embellishments that add to its regal allure. Delicate embroidery, painstakingly crafted with golden threads, traces sinuous patterns along the bodice and cascades down the voluminous skirt.

Exchanging my clothes for the dress, I notice the bodice accentuates my figure with a gentle yet flattering embrace. The neckline, a graceful scoop that frames my collarbones, is encrusted with golden gemstones that sparkle like stars in the night sky. The gemstones are arranged in a delicate filigree pattern, creating an illusion of celestial constellations.

The gown's skirt billows out in opulent layers of silk, each layer catching the light differently, creating a mesmerizing play of shadows and highlights. It flows with a graceful fluidity as if it's an extension of my movements.

I glide through the room, the golden silk of the gown rustling softly with each step, creating a melodic whisper that echoes in harmony with my heartbeat.

As I enter the ballroom, my entrance is nothing short of breathtaking. The gown, bathed in the soft glow of chandeliers, cast reflections that dance like constellations upon the walls. Murmurs of awe ripple through the gathered souls as all eyes turn toward me, their gazes drawn to the luminous fabric.

The ballroom comes alive with an energy of its own as I move through its opulent expanse. Music swirls through the air, and the dance floor reminds me of my time with Netherius.

Thinking back to the time before Nekrojudex, I realize I wasn't living, just existing.

Holding my head high, I stroll past the gawking bystanders across the dancefloor and stop before the dais. The God of the Underworld, a figure cloaked in shifting shadows and crowned with an aura of boundless power, sits upon his throne, his eyes solely on me.

If this was the night I stepped into the palace for the first time, I would have lowered my gaze and addressed him formally. But I can't. After everything we've shared, I can't pretend not to know him.

Holding his stare, I reach my hand out to him.

"What are you doing?" he asks, his teeth clenched.

"I want to know how it feels to dance with the real Netherius," I whisper, so no one else can hear me.

As if moved by a silent command, Otyx rises from his dark throne, his wings unfurling like vast, shadowy blinds.

He descends the steps with a grace that belies the darkness that shrouds him.

I stand still as the God approaches, my heart beating with the anticipation that hangs in the air. The ballroom falls into a hushed silence, and all eyes turn toward the mesmerizing spectacle unfolding—the God of the Underworld extending his hand in my direction.

With a gentle yet deliberate gesture, the God offers his hand to me, and I accept it with a smile. Our hands meet, and in that touch, I feel the energy sizzling between us—a connection that transcends the boundaries of the mortal and the divine.

Together, we move to the center of the ballroom, where the music swells and envelopes us like a passionate embrace. The notes swirl through the air, a haunting but sweet melody that I can't help but sway to. We begin to dance, our movements synchronized, as if we've done this before together in another lifetime.

"Do you know how to dance?" he asks, pressing his hand against my back.

"Actually. I met a Prince once who was an excellent mentor," I answer, looking into his dark eyes. "But that seems like ages ago."

"Good. I hate for you to compare me to another man," he growls, twirling me away from him.

The dance is a mesmerizing display of elegance and power. My golden gown flows like liquid sunlight around me while the God's dark presence seems to envelop us in a dainty embrace. Our steps are precise and fluid, a balance between life and death.

"Have you decided?" he asks, looking down at me.

"A House? No," I say, leaning closer. "But I had time to think about my heart's desire, and I've come to a conclusion."

"Oh, what's that?"

"I don't want to do the right thing. I want to make mistakes. I want to step on other people's toes. I don't want to be afraid of stating my opinion."

"I'm pretty sure you never had a problem with the last one," he teases, his lips' corners curve slightly. "What else?"

"I've wasted so much time making everything possible for everyone else. And I loved it, don't get me wrong. But I want to be selfish. I want to experience how it is to embrace a side of me I didn't know I had."

"Is this your way of asking me to help you?" he growls. As we dance, his wings unfurl further, their shadowy tendrils curling around us like a protective shroud. The darkness emanating from his wings seems to seep into the fabric of the ballroom, casting the world beyond into a sinister darkness.

As the dance reaches its crescendo, he draws me close, his embrace sending warmth through my body. His wings curl around me like a protective cocoon, and we're enveloped in darkness and smoke for a fleeting moment.

"What do you want?" he asks, leaning down to me.

In his embrace, I feel a profound sense of belonging and understanding. I've journeyed through the trials of the Underworld, faced my past, and find myself dancing with the very deity who betrayed me yet always tried to protect me.

"You," I whisper, and darkness swallows me before I can say another word.

THIRTY-FIVE

Avira

"The ball," I say when I open my eyes just to find myself back in my room in the palace.

"It can wait," he says, still holding onto me. "Did you mean what you said?"

For the first time since I laid eyes on Otyx, I can see a faint shimmer of dark irises in the black voids. "I'm not afraid. You can't break me," I answer, resting my hand on his chest. "I still have to get used to those wings, but—"

"I can shapeshift if you prefer Netherius," he says, trying to get out of my grip to make space for his change, but I hold him tight.

"No," I say firmly, taking in the darkness radiating off him. "You're perfect. Besides, I already had him in my dreams."

I chuckle loudly as Otyx raises an eyebrow. "That's why you couldn't look at me? You had a—"

I reach up to cover his mouth. "Yeah, let's never mention that again," I cut in, my cheeks heating.

Fearing I ruined the moment between us, I slowly lift my hand off his face, but he grabs it, turns it over, and kisses the back of it slowly. My eyes are glued to the skin where his lips touch me. It's so innocent, yet it breaks the invisible barrier between us.

Without wasting another second, I stand on my toes and grab his neck with both hands to pull him down to me.

When Netherius visited me in my dream, I didn't know if I'd ever slept with another person before. But now that I have my memories back, I know I wasn't all innocent.

When my lips press against the God's, I can feel his power beneath our touch. It's violent, yet gentle. Consuming, yet soothing.

I expect him to pull away, to tell me I'm mistaken. But I'm pressed against the closet in an instant, his mouth nibbling on my neck with tenderness.

Two souls. That's all we are. Two desperate souls trapped in a world that isn't meant for them.

While most people only know the God's reputation as Death, I've met the true immortal hiding beneath smoke and darkness. And I love what I see.

My breaths come out ragged when he pulls away, darkness seeping through every pore. "Can I make one suggestion?" he asks, slowly unzipping the back of my dress.

I moan as I press myself against him. It's enough of an answer.

"Temptress doesn't suit you," he says, and I feel his fingers gliding over my bare back.

"Is that so?" I ask, looking into his eyes. "Which name do you prefer instead?"

"Conqueress. That's what they should call you," he whispers into my ear as he pushes the gown off my shoulders.

"*Conqueress*?" I ask, weighing the name on my tongue.

"You don't know how long I've waited for this moment," he growls, stepping back to take my naked body in. "You conquered what's left of my heart and an entire Underworld with your presence."

"Then don't wait any longer," I say, stepping out of my gown and closer to him.

When I reach for his skirt, I'm surprised it's already gone. My cheeks flush momentarily when I see the massive erection pointing at me.

"Oh Gods," I mumble as desire washes over me.

"They can't help you now," he chuckles, picking me up as if I'm weightless. Pressing his face into my breasts, he carries me to the bed before letting me down gently.

Slowly, I push myself back, making space for him, and my breath hitches when I watch him crawl after me on all fours.

He's so dark and sexy. I can feel his dominance as he builds himself up above me, but I don't want to be taken the same way Netherius did in my dream. As he leans down to take in my nipple, I press my hand into his chest. It shouldn't be this easy to push a God off, but he follows my command, laying down beside me. His fingers glide over my skin as I turn to face him before I straighten up. His eyes widen when I lift my leg over him and his erection to position myself on top of him.

When my fingers curl around his dick, I'm worried for a moment that he won't fit. But that's a problem I have to deal with once we finally connect. As my hand encloses his cock, I feel his fist close around mine, his knuckles turning white from the pressure as he guides himself in and out of my grip.

Oh, Gods. I can't take it any longer. If I don't have him inside me soon, I will fall over the edge just looking at him masturbating with my hand.

My lower belly burns as I take his growls in. This soul, this God, he's mine. Whatever I want from him, he will do it for me.

With that confirmation, I pull his cock closer and rub his tip over my folds until I find my opening. We both stop breathing for a second before I relax, my legs holding me inches away from his hips, and take him in.

My insides burn as I lower myself, over and over again, to take his length in. He's big. No, massive, and it hurts as my vagina adjusts to his girth. Once the pain subsides, I can't get enough of him. I know I will be sore, but I want to ache. I want to feel his hips slam into me, and his rough hands knit my breasts until they feel raw. I want to ride him like there's no tomorrow.

His hands, shadowy and warm, grip me forcefully by my hips to move my body to his liking. He groans as he lifts me up and down, and I moan, throwing my head back to take him in deeper and deeper until my ass claps against his hips. At this point, it's impossible to know if it's him who's moving me or if it's me controlling our pace. His groans reverberate through me as he fastens our pace, and warmth builds up in my core.

He's fucking perfect.

"You're such a bad girl," he whispers, driving harder into me.

I'm whining in pleasure, unable to answer. I'm so close. If he keeps this pace up, we won't finish together.

I wince when he sits up beneath me, his arm curling around my waist while his other drives over my nipples. "I want to see your face when you come undone," he growls, moving me on his dick again.

His warm breath caresses my face as he leans in to kiss me, still driving into me relentlessly. When our lips touch, my muscles burst into flames. I feel the warmth spreading through my lower body as an orgasm washes over me. The moment I open my mouth to let the ecstasy he has been building up inside me out, I feel his cock throbbing, and he joins my moans.

He keeps moving me until every ounce of his pleasure is pressed out of him. Together, we collapse on the bed, panting.

THIRTY-SIX

Avira

"What's wrong?" I ask as Otyx tilts his head to the ceiling after he covers me with a thin blanket to keep me warm. I've seen that stare before. It's like he can hear through the surface's crust when he's needed.

"Besides collecting souls, it's also my responsibility to even the scales," he says, narrowing his eyes. "Now that you remember your past, you might know Crymzon runs on magic."

"And?"

"They use it to cheat death. And every few thousand years, when the number of uncollected souls threatens to tip the scales, I must find a way to obtain them."

I shake my head. "I don't understand."

"When I had to leave after you found out about my shapeshifting ability, I was called to the surface to secure the remaining uncollected souls. That means, for the next unforeseeable future,

I only have to go occasionally to the surface when a mortal dies of natural causes."

My mind throws me back to the clothing room. "I saw the armor."

"Usually, I never had a problem with Crymzon's ruler to collect their debt. They didn't hand them over freely, but they also never held a grudge. That's not the case with the new Queen," he says, still listening to something I can't hear.

"What happened to King Obsidian?" I ask, trying to recall all the Kings and Queens of my time.

"His demise came from his own daughter. The same daughter who's now leading Crymzon."

My brows draw together when I try to understand what he's saying. "She killed her father?"

"And brother," he answers, sitting up in bed.

I follow his movement. "What is she doing now? Can you see or hear her?"

He clicks his tongue. "She's trying to summon me. But it's not her who's on my mind. It's her Soulmate. I can feel his expiration coming close."

I look up at the ceiling, concentrating on hearing whatever he can, to no avail. "What does she want from you?"

"Revenge. After taking half of her people, she's trying to get to me. What she doesn't realize is that through my power, her Soulmate is still alive."

"This is all going too fast," I say, moving my hands to slow him down.

"You might not know much about the Soulmate Connection Crymzonians share," he says, standing up. "After all the heartbreak the Queen has been through, she finally accepted her Soulmate after a thallium sword pierced his heart. I thought mending his wound with my power would ease her rage and heartache so she wouldn't have to lose him, too. But it didn't. And even though I've completed my job and withdrew all the souls I sent to finish the job for me, she's trying to find a way to take me down."

I laugh. "But that's impossible. You are immortal. You are a God."

"Nothing is impossible," he says, and his skirt reappears with a snap of his fingers.

"So, what are you going to do? Are you going to kill her?"

Otyx chuckles. "I can't. It's not her time."

"But what if—"

Then, as if a phantom of the night, he begins to fade before my eyes. At first, it's imperceptible—a subtle shifting of contours, a gradual vanishing of form. My heart quickens, my eyes widening with disbelief as I witness the inexplicable.

Panic surges through my veins as I reach out to touch him, my fingers passing through the empty space where he stood just a moment ago. My breath catches in my throat, and I recoil, my mind grappling with the impossible truth.

This can't be real. It has to be a cruel trick. I've seen him use a portal, but nothing could have prepared me for this vanishing act.

"That's not funny. You can come back now," I say with trembling hands. I wait for another moment. Leaping out of bed, my pulse races with frantic urgency. I fumble for some clothes, my thoughts consumed by a single, desperate impulse—I need to find him.

But just as I'm about to bolt for the door, Otyx reappears before me as suddenly as he vanished. He stands there, a bewildered expression upon his face, as if he, too, had been caught in the throes of an unexplainable mystery.

My breaths come in rapid gasps as I stare at him, my heart still pounding with the remnants of fear and confusion. "What-what just happened?" I stammer, my voice quivering.

Otyx, his features a mix of bewilderment and concern, steps closer to me. That's when I see it.

His chest, once smooth and muscular, is marred and damaged. Jagged cuts and holes appear on its surface like a network of lightning strikes, branching out from the center of a gaping hole. His skin is charred and blackened in some areas with deep gouges and splintered rock fragments.

"I don't know," he admits, his eyes searching my face for answers as he holds his chest.

"Lay down, I'm getting help," I say, slowly directing him to the bed. On the outside, I try to stay calm and collected, but on the inside, anger and fear rip me apart. "Don't move," I whisper, taking in his injuries again before I bolt out the door, screaming for help.

THIRTY-SEVEN

Avira

Where are all the souls when you need them? Running through the palace, I keep repeating the exact words. *Help! I need a healer. Help!*

I don't even know if it's possible to heal a God. Until now, I didn't even know they could be injured.

"Mordecai," I scream from an open window, hoping he will hear me. But even if he shows up, what is he supposed to do?

Running as fast as I can, I return to the only place I know—the House of Lust. Breaking through the door, I don't halt when I see Isabella on the throne, watching other souls engulfed in their sin.

"Sword!" she yells when she recognizes me. I freeze when one of her sinners holds a blade in my direction.

"I'm not here to take your place," I answer, lifting my hands.

"Is that what the God whispered into your ear? To come here, looking helpless, just to stab me in the back."

I shake my head vigorously. "I'm here to save him. Please, I need your help!" I answer, running to the dais, but I'm met with her blade pointing at me.

"For the last time, I'm not here to fight. Otyx is dying," I scream, shaking my head. "Please, help!"

The laugh reverberating out of her chest sends me over the edge. "I'm not a moron. The Gods can't die. And now, try your theatrical performance in another palace before I come down there and cut you down."

Replaying our last encounters, I realize she didn't come to apologize for selecting me. She came to apologize because she knew what my mother put me through. After passing the first two trials, she figured out that there was a possibility that I would end up as the champion. She only sought me out because she wanted to save her own ass. And she did it again when she locked me in her cage.

"If you're not out of here by three—"

"You knew my past, didn't you?" I ask, studying her long hair and pale face.

"Stop changing the subject."

She might not realize that by dodging my question, I get my confirmation.

Fear grips my heart, a primal, all-consuming terror that threatens to engulf me. Otyx, my source of comfort and solace, is slipping through my fingers, torn away by the laughter of the interloper.

As Isabella laughs again, a transformation takes hold of me—a metamorphosis from fear to a seething, consuming hatred. It courses through my veins like molten lava, burning away any trace of vulnerability. My very essence shifts, and in that moment, white wings erupt from my shoulder blades through my shirt, unfurling like the wings of a vengeful angel.

For ninety-seven years, I didn't know who I was. For all those years, I forgot that I'm the daughter of Caecilia, the Queen of Starstrand. As a Princess, I had wings because that's who I was, a Winged Warrior. And now, down here in the Underworld, I'm still the same.

Mother of Lust, oblivious to the tempest brewing within me, continues to laugh, her voice a mocking melody that pierces my soul, fueling my fury's flames.

With a surge of anger, I propel myself forward. My hands shoot out, grabbing her by the shoulders with a vice-like grip. The laughter ceases abruptly, replaced by wide-eyed shock as she drops her sword.

My rage burns like a white-hot fire as my wings envelop us, casting a pall of light around her.

"You dare...," I hiss, my voice trembling with a blend of hatred and betrayal. My grip tightens, fingers digging into Isabella's shoulders, my nails like claws. "You dare to mock what's mine?"

Mother of Lust, now trapped within my grasp, trembles with fear. Her eyes meet mine, and in that moment, she understands the depths of the rage she ignited. "That's impossible. Your wings can't grow in the Underworld," she says, her eyes zigzagging between them.

I don't care how I managed to get my wings back. All I know is that I feel whole again.

"Please let me go," she says as I flap them, lifting her off her throne.

The room quivers with the intensity of our confrontation as if the very fabric of the Underworld itself is responding to my wrath.

"I came here to ask you for help," I say through clenched teeth. "But everything you care about is yourself. I didn't come here to take your throne. But you know what? It's kinda growing on me."

My newfound power crackles like lightning in the charged air. I must make her understand the consequences of provoking a heart consumed by love and hatred. It only takes a few beats for us to reach the ceiling.

"Please, let me go," Isabella pleads, holding onto me for dear life.

"As you please," I growl, releasing her shoulders. I watch Isabella's eyes widen when she realizes what I've done. But I don't wait for her to hit the ground. Instead, I use my new wings to fly through the open door back to Shadowmyre to check on Otyx.

With some luck, she might survive the fall. If not, there's one less decision I have to make because that would make me the new Head of Lust.

THIRTY-EIGHT

AVIRA

The door flies off its hinges as I break through it.

"Slow down," Ruby yells as Mordecai shields her from splintered wooden pieces.

Without saying a word, I run to the bed, and when I see Otyx breathing heavily, another wave of fear washes over me.

"He can't die," I whisper, trying to reach his hand, but I almost erupt when I see someone else touch his chest.

"You need to give her some space," Ruby says, grabbing me by the shoulders to push me back. "Oh, Gods. What happened to you?" she asks, looking over my shoulder at my wings.

I press my weight against her to get through. "Not now. We need to save him."

"Maeve is doing everything she can to recover all the rock fragments in his chest. But I need you to stay calm," she says, hugging me. "Take her out of here," she says over my shoulder, and when a set of claws curl around my waist, I scream.

"No. I need to stay with him. I can't go."

Ruby holds me by the shoulders. "Avira. I promise you, he's in expert hands. But you can't watch this."

Fighting against Mordecai's grip with all my might, I watch as he drags me to the door before squeezing through it again.

"I've gotten better," he says as he makes it through without tearing the wall down.

"He needs me," I scream, clawing at his nails.

"No. He needs prayers," he answers, covering the door.

I shake my head. "What did you say?"

"I said *he needs prayers*."

"You're a genius," I say, recalling my conversation with Netherius, well, Otyx, close to the Darklands.

He said he's bound to this realm because no mortal worships him. But he's wrong. I'm not a soul doomed for eternity to live here. I still possess my color because he took me prisoner alive instead of claiming my soul and killing me. I'm mortal. Maybe one living soul isn't enough to strengthen him, but it's all I have left.

"Where are you going?" Mordecai yells behind me as I run down the corridor.

"I know how to help him," I whisper, rounding the corner to find a way to the throne room.

I stand before the imposing dais of the God of the Underworld. Behind it, hidden out of view, lies a small, carved stone basin hewn from the same dark stone as the dais. In my trembling hand, I hold a sharp piece of rock I found in the corridor that used to belong to my wall.

My heart pounds so hard in my chest that I can't hear anything but the blood rushing through my veins.

"I pledge my life to you," I whisper, my voice echoing in the cavernous chamber. As I pick up the rock, my gaze never wavers from the black stone before me. My eyes are fixed upon the basin that awaits my offering.

I puncture my finger with a steady hand, allowing a single drop of blood to fall. It strikes the stone with a hauntingly melodic sound, a note of submission and devotion that resonates through the chamber. The liquid spreads across the stone's surface like a luminous pool, its glow deepening with each passing moment.

As the liquid seeps into the stone, I feel the connection forming, a link between my mortal soul and the deity of the Underworld. It's as if a bridge was built between my world and the realm of Shadowmyre.

A surge of power courses through me. My senses seem to expand, allowing me to perceive the underlying currents of the Underworld—the ebb and flow of its enigmatic energies. I feel the weight of my pledge, a commitment that binds me to Otyx.

The dais, the basin, and the black stone all resonate with a subtle energy, a manifestation of the God's acknowledgment of my devotion. I've offered myself willingly to the deity who never had a mortal worshiping him, and in return, I've become a part of him.

When I close my eyes, I can feel him, and with every passing second, I can feel his heartbeat strengthening.

I did it. I saved him.

Rising off the floor, I turn around and startle when I see a man standing in the middle of the throne room. He seems disoriented. When our eyes meet, his brows furrow. "Where am I?"

His brown curls fall into his face as my eyes rest on the black liquid seeping through his shirt.

"Don't be afraid. I can help you," I say, raising my hands to signal I'm not a threat. Careful not to scare him, I descend the stairs until I stand before him.

"You don't understand. My Queen needs me. I can't be here," he says, looking around.

Queen.

There are only three Queens to choose from in the mortal world, and two are currently not in my favor.

He revolts when I come closer. When our skin touches, I feel his desires, past, and everything he's done before dying. It's like I experienced his entire life in less than a minute.

Is this what Otyx feels when he collects a soul? Did he see my past like I've seen this man's?

"Do you feel better?" I ask, releasing him.

I watch as his tanned skin slowly turns gray. I'm not the God of the Underworld with the ability to erase his memories, but somehow it worked. Slowly, I can see his past separate from him until he's merely a shell of who he used to be.

"Tell me your name," I say, tilting my head.

He shakes his head as if he can't remember it. But I've heard it in his memories. I listened to the way the Crymzon Queen addressed him as Khaos.

"She chose violence, and *Khaos* she'll get," I whisper, and the smile on his face tells me he's ready to start his afterlife without a single memory of who he used to be.

ABOUT THE AUTHOR

C.K. Franziska is the author of the finished A *Speck of Darkness* series, and her second series, The Crymzon Chronicles. She is the wife of a traveler, as well as the mother of two mini versions of herself and way too many pets. In her spare time, she is also a photographer, traveler, full-time entertainer, and animal lover. She does her best writing at night, at the beach listening to the waves, or while camping. C.K. loves to play make-believe, transporting readers to a place where the heroes have to step out of the seemingly endless cycle of family curses, where the magic is as beautiful and untamable as we think, and where every person deserves to be celebrated.